Predator X

C.J. Waller

www.severedpress.com

ISBN: 978-1-925047-73-8

Chapter One

They say there are no true wildernesses left to explore. You talk to those extreme survival types and they even mock places like Antarctica as for mere novices. Maybe they're right about that. I mean, you can take a five star cruise to see the penguins nowadays. But they're wrong about the wilderness thing. They are there; they're just a bastard to get to. We know less about our oceans than we do about the moon, but that's a wealth of knowledge compared to what we know about the deep places of the Earth. That's where the cool kids hang out. In caves.

I'm not a cool kid. I'm a sedimentologist, and that's about as glamorous as it sounds. But I do like caves. So when we were fracking for shale gas on the Tuvan border and we broke through to a vast subterranean network of caves, I was amongst the first to volunteer to go down and have a look.

Training was pretty brutal. The guys who run it don't piss about, and they can't. One false move and you're dead. It really is as simple as that. I thought about dropping out lots of times, but curiosity is a strange beast. It's more powerful than terror, for one thing. Let's just say a thousand bad decisions in various horror movies all of a sudden make a great deal of sense to me.

I wanted to be in the Alpha team, to be one of the first to experience things, but I'm a scientist, not a survivalist. They picked the team best suited to sort out the route, and at first, things seemed to be going pretty well. They sent us back information via a set of radio relays and basic video feed: some tight spots, but nothing insurmountable. Then we got a tantalising hint of something new, something we totally didn't expect – a huge inland sea, cut off from the surface for millennia. That did it. I knew I had to get down there.

But after that – nothing.

We still don't know what happened to the Alpha team, but we're going to find out.

* * * * *

Caves are sacred places. They're a bit like churches, or libraries. You don't shout. Part of that is for safety reasons - loud sounds have a nasty habit of dislodging rocks, which in turn bang into other rocks, and before you know it you're crushed by a hundred tons of the stuff – but a bigger reason is to do with the atmosphere. It's heavy. Not like hippy-heavy-maaan, but like actually, physically heavy. It can be hard to breathe down here. Thank the Lord (or at least those lovely technicians at the Fujiyama Corporation, anyway) for inventing a decent kinetic two-for-one air filtration and light system. Because that's the other thing about caves. They're dark. Like pitch black, can't see your hand in front of your face dark. There's no light down here. Light has never been down here. But that doesn't mean life isn't.

That came as quite a surprise. We were expecting to find some traces of life, you know, algae and the like, but the sheer number of species – all of them new to science, or so we expect – is staggering. It's a shame they're all of the fucking terrifying kind – spiders, centipedes, weird worms with mouths full of hooks and other such nasties – but it really does go to show you that life will indeed find a way.

"For Chrissakes, Meg!" A voice hisses out of the darkness. I look up, pen in hand. It's Marcus, hassling me again. Now there's a surprise. "You're always fucking writing. We have cameras to record this shit. You don't need to scribble."

He grins. He might sound like a total arsehole, but Marcus is okay once you get used to him. He's part of the survival team. He was supposed to join the Alpha team, but injury kept him out of that gig, and as much as he protests, I think he's pretty glad it kept him off that team, considering everything.

We've been here for a couple of hours now. There's a bastard chimney to traverse, and Nik and Janos wanted to go first. Of course, Alpha team have already rigged it, but they're both aware we're not all experts at this, so they're going first, just in case.

I'm beginning to feel a bit concerned. We've had to wait about before, but never for this long. I find myself peering into the never-ending darkness of the pit ahead, trying to figure out if that's the dim-light of their kinetic torches, or just my eyes giving up and my brain filling in the gaps.

Even Marcus is quiet now. Fi has her eyes closed – how can she sleep like that? It took me ages to acclimate. I suppose she's had more experience. Brendan, on the other hand, is like me, scribbling away, noting everything down. If anything, he's even worse. It's a cave ecologist's wet dream down here. I think if we discover one more new species, he might explode.

Small echoes filter up from below. Even though I know it's only Nick and Janos returning, my heart jitters. No one talks about it, but it's obvious the disappearance of Alpha Team is on everyone's mind. No one knows what happened to them. We're hoping someone just dropped the equipment... but why then have they not returned? No. Not going to think about that. Not yet. Not until –

I screw my eyes up and swallow hard. Why am I even thinking about this? Just concentrate on what you're doing. There's enough to worry about without all of… that.

A figure pops its head over the edge of the ridge: Janos. He looks pretty grim, but that doesn't worry me. He always looks pretty grim in a Hollywood hard-man kind of way. When I first met him, I half expected him to speak in tired clichés and demand people make his day, but in reality, he's a serious man who only really speaks when necessary.

"Nikolai has stayed below to steady the rope," he says. It sounds like a funeral announcement. "The going isn't easy, but it is still better than we expected." He turns to Marcus. "You should go first, then one of the scientists, then Fiona, and then the other scientist. I shall go last." With that, he nods and settles himself on the edge of the chimney. He knows no one will argue with him, not about this. Janos might be a miserable son of a bitch sometimes, but he has an instinct about caves we've all learned to trust.

Marcus agrees to go first, and then volunteers me. "I ain't gonna stare at Brendan's arse all the way down," he grins. I used to be bothered by his banter, but not now. He's harmless.

My stomach swoops as Janos helps me manoeuvre myself over the edge. Apart from Marcus's headlamp ten feet below me, there is no light - I might as well be stepping off into the infinite. Janos shows me my hand holds, and I'm off, using the carefully placed guide ropes to help me down.

Janos wasn't kidding. This is, without a doubt, a bitch of a climb. Below me, I can hear Marcus muttering under his breath. I rarely see his headlamp head-on when I glance down – I guess his joke about preferring my arse over Brendan's has long been forgotten now he's worrying about where to put his feet.

My legs are screaming at me. I'm fitter than I've ever been, but it doesn't matter, every climb is a punishment. You'd also think going down would be easier, but it isn't. Going up means, you know where you're going. Down? That's largely guesswork, or so it feels.

I take in a deep breath and pause for a moment before I unclip my safety harness to transfer it to the next series of ropes. This is the bit I always hate, the bit I never think I'll ever get used to. Even though it takes but a second, I can't help but shake the feeling that it would only take a second to slip. I only let my breath go when I snap the D-ring closed and give it a tug. Safe again. Well, safer.

I glance up. Three little lights dance above me as the others join in the descent. The air tastes strange down here, cold and metallic. The walls are dry. We're too deep for ground water, and so the prelim reports of an inland sea came as a huge surprise – I mean, how the hell did it form if it hadn't percolated through the rock? But that's the exciting thing. It didn't percolate.

It's always been here.

I continue to edge my way down, my belly now fizzing. I can't help but wonder if we're close. We're mostly using guesswork – we have the Alpha team's marks to follow and that is basically that. GPS doesn't work down here – the rock is too thick and there's a background level of radiation that, whilst harmless to us (pretty much; I wouldn't want to spend months down here if I wanted to have kids at some point), it messes with most of our electrical equipment, which kind of unnerves me.

"Okay, we're nearing the bottom now," Marcus calls up. Good. My arms have joined my legs in a rendition of The Screaming Chorus, and I'm just about ready to let go.

"Hit bottom!" Another call, followed by a furious whisper that travels far easier in the dead air. "Where the fuck is Nik?"

My stomach sinks. We're nearing our goal – and to where Alpha team vanished. The last thing our collective nerves need is to lose a team member of our own.

I scramble down the last 10 feet, trying to concentrate on what I am doing but failing miserably. My fingers slip and I slide down the last 5 feet, scraping my hands. Only the thick material of my survival suit protects my knees. I hit the bottom far faster than intended, and my legs crumple under me.

Marcus is nowhere to be seen.

A black dread seizes me. First Nik, then Marcus – what next?

Fi lands next to me as I find my feet. She doesn't seem all that concerned that Nik and Marcus have all but disappeared. Instead, she stalks off into the gloom and ducks her head down.

"Nik?" she says.

"Yep!" comes the answer.

"Tight?"

"Yep."

Fi grins. "Good."

Rather than cheer me, this exchange makes my stomach sink even further. The guys haven't disappeared, they've just gone to investigate the route, which seems to end in a blank cliff face.

Until you notice the crack at the bottom, that is.

Cavers call them 'flatteners'. I call them nightmares, and I don't mean that as in 'difficult'. I mean 'nightmares' as in 'tit-shrivelling terrifying'. They are the one aspect of caves I don't think I'll ever be able to fully cope with, and if it wasn't for the potential of something truly awe-inspiring on the other side, I don't think I could do it.

Brendan and Janos have now joined us. Fi strips off her pack and pushes it into the crack. She then lies flat and wriggles underneath. That's why they're called 'flatteners', by the way, because that's the only way you can get through them – flat on your stomach.

Brendan goes next. He might not have the survival credentials the others do, but he has far more experience dealing with flatteners, and caves in general, than I do. He strips his pack and off he wriggles. I feel my heart clamber up into my throat and I swallow convulsively. I am not going to panic. It's safe. Four other people have gone before me, and they're okay. So no panicking.

I slowly pull off my backpack and sink to the floor. I'm feeling light headed now, like I've had one bevvy too many. I push my pack forward and fight down the urge to grab the top of my head to stop it from floating off.

"Are you all right?"

Janos is kneeling beside me, looking concerned. He places a steady hand on my back. "I shall be there with you. Do not worry. I shall not let you get stuck."

His sincerity helps. I'm still on the verge of hyperventilating when I lie down and peer into the pitch-black of the crack, but Janos' presence keeps me from losing it completely. He might be a bit of a killjoy most of the time, but right now, I am grateful for him, for his steadiness, for his seriousness. Marcus would joke; Fi would gloat; Nik would shrug, but Janos? Janos will keep me safe. Plus, he's like twice my size, and if he thinks he can squeeze through this gap, then it should be a cake walk for me.

"Remember," he says, cutting through my rising panic. "Do not touch anything Nik has sprayed yellow. Keep breathing and keep going forwards. You will be fine."

I take in a deep breath and stretch out into the flattener, pushing my pack ahead of me. I twist my head so my hard hat doesn't get wedged, cringing when I hear the scrape of rock against plastic. I inch forwards, focusing on my back. Behind me, a sudden flare of light tells me Janos has joined me. He taps my boot.

"Yellow ahead."

I drag my pack a little to the right, and sure enough, there's a splash of fluorescent yellow spray paint on the rock. I shuffle sideways, avoiding it. Nik's a cautious guy. It could be safe to touch it, but I don't want to be the one to test his judgement.

Despite the flattener opening out enough for me to raise my head a bit, it feels tighter than ever in here. The floaty feeling comes back. I blink in an attempt at clearing it, but all I can think is how much rock there currently is above my head. They say they've suspended all fracking operations until we've investigated, but that doesn't mean the damage hasn't already been done. One false move and I'm a fucking pancake - or worse, trapped, cocooned forever in a tomb of limestone, three miles down, where no one can hear me scream, and even if they could, they wouldn't be able to do anything about it.

"Keep going," Janos says.

I dig my toes into the floor and push onwards. He's right. I have to keep going. But I can't move. I try again, but I'm stuck. Stuck fast – stuck under the rock, unable to escape. My breathing quickens and I try to raise my head, which smashes into the ceiling above me – a ceiling that is crushing down upon me, trapping me, suffocating me-

"Don't panic." Janos says, cutting through my building terror. "Your boot strap is caught on a nodule."

I feel him fumble at my foot, followed by a sense of pressure released. I try again, and miraculously, I am able to propel myself forward. Light floods the gap and a hand stretches out. It is Marcus, checking our progress.

"You all right, chick?" he asks as he drags me from the flattener. "You look like you've seen a ghost."

I try to answer him, but I can't. I'm shaking too much. Janos scrambles out behind me and shoulders his pack.

"She did well," he says and stalks past me to take his customary place at the head of our team.

It takes me a little while to shake off the claustrophobia of the flattener. What doesn't help is that I know we have to return this way to get back. It almost makes being stuck down here forever a palatable experience.

Marcus is back behind me now. I don't know why. He seems to like being around me, for some reason. Maybe he just likes having someone around who he can feel superior to. Well, it's either that or he fancies me. That doesn't make me feel any better, though. He's got a wife and three kids, and there's no way I'm being the bitch who splits up that happy family. Not that I'd want to. Marcus is hardly my type.

He's blathering on about something, but I'm not really listening. Why would I be when there's so much wonder surrounding me? This part of the cave is something else; that much is for sure. Brendan keeps pausing to study the rock surface, and every now and again, he shakes his head, his expression caught perfectly between excitement and bewilderment. I don't blame him. I'm pretty excited about it all, too. The walls are covered in a strange slime – probably some kind of chemotrophic bacteria or something along those lines given the lack of sunlight down here – and it glows. As in 'eldritch grotto' glows. It's a weird, bluish green light that is unlike anything I have ever experienced outside of a rave, and it serves absolutely no biological purpose whatsoever, given that everything down here has evolved in pitch-blackness. It's like the cave wants us down here.

The going is pretty easy now – a few large boulders to scramble over and one partially choked bolt hole are our only real obstacles. There's evidence of the rocks being moved about, which in turn makes my thoughts shift to the Alpha Team. I'm not surprised that we haven't come across much in the way of evidence of their passage – the motto of any caver worth his or her salt is 'take nothing but experience, leave nothing but memory' – and considering just how important this discovery might be, they've even got us shitting in special plastic bags that desiccates everything down to almost nothing so we can carry all and any waste back home – but I still cant' help feel a little twinge of something that skirts the edge of worry. There's no evidence they were here, but that also means there's no evidence of what happened to them, and that's playing on my mind. Are we about to walk into the same trap they did?

"Fucking hell…" Nik breathes up ahead. Behind him, Fi is shaking her head in disbelief. I clamber up the small section of scree and join them.

Fucking hell indeed.

We knew the Alpha Team had discovered something huge when we first received their footage. Their reactions also spoke of their awe at their discovery, but just like most wonders of the world, nothing beats experiencing it first hand.

The ledge we are standing on drops down about fifteen feet onto what I can only describe as a beach, covered with a glittering, black sand. The nearby cliff sides are all covered in that weird glowing chemotrophic bacteria, making the whole thing look like some kind faerie underworld of legend. But that's not what's making us swear and our jaws drop.

The sea does that.

The first time I went to America, I witnessed the majesty of Lake Champlain. Being a Brit, I thought I knew what a lake looked like (Windermere, if you're curious), but when I first saw Champlain, I realised what I'd seen before were mere puddles.

This body of water exceeds that.

"How far do you think it goes?" Marcus asks. Beside me, Brendan shrugs.

"It could just be a trick of the, uh, light, but we'd hypothesised the body of water down here rivalled the Black Sea in size, and it looks like we might have been right."

The Black Sea. Yeah, that feels an appropriate comparison. It stretches out as far as any of us can see. Beyond this cave, there is nothing – just a huge expanse of inky water. It's eerie; on the surface you have the horizon to help you judge distance, but here there is nothing, making it both daunting and claustrophobic at the same time. The nearest analogy I can think of might be looking into the vast depths of space. A strange sense of vertigo overtakes me, and for a moment, I feel like I'm floating. I reach out and grab the nearest thing to me, which happens to be Janos.

"Dr Stoker," he says and stops me from pitching forwards. "Are you all right?"

I nod and swallow hard, but can't trust myself to speak. Not yet, anyway.

We begin our descent one after the other. As usual, Nik goes first, declaring the climb a piece of piss – lots of hand holes in the pitted surface. Janos hangs back with me, and I'm a little miffed.

Has he been told to keep an eye on me? I won't lie – his solid presence is a comfort, so I don't complain.

Nik is right; the climb is pretty easy, and before long we are all standing on that strange beach, staring at the sea. The air has a briny tang to it, and the glowing bacteria forms thick mats on the rocks nearest the shoreline, outlining the seashore in phosphorescence. Brendan stoops down and cups his hand in the water before swilling a little in his mouth. I'm not sure how wise that is, but I'm not here to stop him.

"Yep. Salt," he says. "And warmer than I was expecting. Could be there's some hydrothermal activity down there."

"In a sedimentary cave system?" Fi asks. She doesn't do much to disguise her disdain. I don't think she likes Brendan all that much.

"Depends," I say, feeling the need to defend my fellow scientist. "The upper part of the system is sedimentary, but if this body of water is deep enough, it could just be overlaying a geologically active zone. It isn't unheard of."

"But that would mean it could be thousands of feet deep."

I shrug. "It could be."

"How long do you think it has been isolated from the surface?" Nik asks.

Again, I shrug. "I don't know. They were fracking Jurassic shale, so in theory, we could be looking at, what, one hundred and sixty million years?"

Marcus lets out a low whistle. "One hundred and sixty million? Are you serious?"

"Well, I'm not a paleobiologist… but yeah, we could be."

"So, if anything is living in there, it could have been cut off from the rest of evolution for nearly two hundred million years?"

"Yeah."

"If anything is living in there," Fi says.

"Actually, the chances of there being something in there are pretty good," says Brendan. "If the presence of bacteria indicates this system is still biologically active, there's no reason why not. Samples from other such isolated bodies of water indicate that life is quite capable of thriving independently of the outside world.

Take Lake Vostok, for example. They went looking for bacteria and found fish."

"You think there might be fish in there?" Marcus says.

"Could be." Brendan grins, and I can't help smile. His enthusiasm is infectious. "Who knows?"

Chapter Two

It doesn't take us long to sort out a rudimentary base camp. Brendan and I are left to sort out the science shit (as Marcus calls it) whilst the others go off in pairs to scout out the rest of the 'beach', but their feigned nonchalance doesn't hide their true intentions. I know what they're really doing.

We haven't found any evidence of the Alpha Team's whereabouts apart from a lone boot-print near the water's edge. What's also pretty baffling is that the beach we're studying right now bears no resemblance to the area the Alpha Team were filming in when their feed mysteriously gave up. So either we've taken a pretty huge wrong turn, or this is not where they ended up (which, in turn, throws up even more questions, starting with 'who the hell left the boot print?'). Problem is, apart from the sea, there isn't anywhere left to go.

Preliminary geological samples indicate that a lot of the rocks around here are Palaeozoic in origin, which means that this area has been pretty much geologically stable for a hell of a long time. There's minimal folding and I'm pretty stoked to find a couple of exquisite trilobite fossils that I know my palaeontologist buddies will be all over if I can justify taking them out of this system. Brendan is all but hopping around in glee, taking samples of the bacteria and setting little traps in the occasional rock-pool located at the water's edge.

"Don't you get it?" he asks at my puzzled looks. "It means this is a tidal system. It really is a sea."

Despite everything, I grin back at him. Yes, Brendan, I get it. This whole place is pretty much the definition of awesome.

After a couple of hours, we're all together, debating our next move. It's weird. Now we're here, we're not entirely sure what to do. We've kind of confirmed an Alpha team sighting, if spotting a lone boot print counts as a sighting… now what?

Fi tries to send our report back, but the feed is screwed. Maybe that's really what happened to the Alpha Team. But that only raises even more questions than answers. If the feed failed, fine – but then where are they?

I gaze over the cold, black water of the subterranean sea. Despite there being no breeze, its surface ripples. In the weird half-light of the bacteria, it's eerily beautiful and totally disconcerting. Occasionally I hear a splash, which sets off the old imagination. Cut off from the surface for anything up to one hundred and sixty million years… What the hell could be down there? And do we really want to find out?

"Are you all right?" It's Janos, playing again at being our group's daddy.

I nod. "Just wondering."

"Wondering what?"

"What might be down there. How things might be different – if anything survived to be different, of course…"

He grimaces, which is his way of smiling.

"Could be anything," he says.

Yep, Janos – you said it.

"Hang on... That's weird" We focus our attention on Brendan. He's using the low lights, to scan the surface of the water, their oversized frames making him look strangely insectile. "The glow extends above the water over there. Like there is some kind of… of outcrop, or something."

We glance at each other. We don't need to say anything to know we're all thinking the same thing.

That could be where the Alpha Team ended up.

"We should go look," says Marcus. Nik gives him a disdainful look.

"Maybe we should spend a little more time than a couple of hours establishing ourselves here first-"

"Establishing ourselves for what?" Marcus says. "This cave is pretty much it. There aren't any more caves, no pipes, no chimneys – nothing. This is a dead end. And besides, why did we hump the inflatable along if we weren't going to use it?"

He's got a point. Although far lighter than most domestic inflatables, the rubber dinghy still weighs a tonne. It seems stupid to bring it and not use it, especially when it was brought with the sole purpose of studying this body of water as extensively as possible. But, at the same time, I can see Nik's point, too. I don't know what it is, but there's definitely something sinister about this sea. It's probably nothing more than it being so damn old, and having been undiscovered for so long… but for all its beauty, it feels hostile, truly untamed and untameable.

We argue for a bit, and in the end, it is decided that we'll spend a bit longer taking a few samples – mainly water ones, alongside a few chips of rock (that whole 'take nothing but experience' thing is really ingrained) before we prep ourselves for exploring the water in a little more detail.

"So how deep is it?" Fi asks, as she unpacks the small yellow square that will magically inflate to form a four-person boat.

Brendan shrugs. "Without getting in there? I don't know, but I can try to find out."

He unpacks a length of long line and ties a rock to one end. Above the rock, he then attaches a flare. We watch him as he wades out into the water, grinning like a five year old being allowed to sit up front in a fire engine for the first time. Which is ironic, considering I am suddenly gripped by an overwhelming desire to tell him to get out of the water, no don't argue, just get the fuck out! I have to shake myself out of it – yes, it's dark and creepy and weird, but this is not the 1980s, nor is it Camp fucking Crystal, so get a grip. He manages about ten feet before he's up to his waist. We can barely see him against the backdrop of the black water until he cracks the flare and lights the whole place in a demon-flash of crimson, turning the water around him a blood red.

He drops the flare into the water. It sinks and then disappears. All that is left is a red glow as it descends, until it finally disappears from our view entirely.

After a few minutes, Brendan winds the line back in and wades back over to us, shaking his head.

"Well?" Nik asks.

"It's deep," Brendan says. "There's fifty foot of line there and I never once felt it hit anything. The ledge just drops off, straight down."

"Like a trench," I say.

"Like a what?" Fi asks.

"A trench. Straight down. Like when you get to the edge of a reef and then it just drops away."

Brendan nods. "Yeah – exactly. The water coming up from it is pretty cold, too, which indicates it's deep."

"How deep?" Nik asks.

"Dunno. Could be a hundred, could be a thousand... hell, it could be more. Without proper equipment, your guess is as good as mine."

"So we may have discovered a subterranean sea that is thousands of feet deep?" Fi asks.

Brendan shrugs. "Maybe."

"Awesome." Fi grins. "Dibs on being first in the dinghy."

***

The boat takes just under a minute to inflate. Nik's going to row us over – the little red paddles are a bit naff, but he's pretty sure they should do the job, especially since the water looks calm. It's decided that Marcus, Brendan and Fi should go over first, and then he'll come back and pick up me, Janos and the bulk of the equipment if it looks like the boat can handle it.

There is much ribbing and laughing as the four of them wedge themselves in the tiny raft. For a minute, it looks doubtful it'll actually float, but once they're settled, Nik begins the precarious journey across the water, towards the glow.

Janos and I don't speak, we just watch the lights from their headlamps twinkle on the surface of the water. They soon dwindle to pinpricks, tiny shafts of feeble white in the infinite blackness of the cavern. I shiver. Like I said before, I'm not hugely experienced when it comes to caves, but I'm finding the sheer enormity of this cavern even more daunting than the various chimneys, tubes and flatteners I've been forced to endure getting here. I never thought that would be the case, so it just goes to show, you never can tell.

There's a shout in the distance, and immediately, Janos is on tenterhooks.

"Nik?" he calls out.

"What the-?" comes back.

There is the sound of splashing, and a single headlamp whips back and forth. Janos runs forward into the water, but I'm rooted to the spot, my blood thundering in my ears.

Finally, the little yellow inflatable can be seen again. Janos grabs its painter and pulls it into shallower water.

Nik looks white, his eyes huge.

"What happened?" Janos asks.

"I don't know," Nik says. "Something… something hit the boat. Made it rock. I thought it might, you know, capsize…"

"Probably a stray current," Janos says.

Nik nods, but doesn't look all that convinced. "Yeah, you're probably right. I mean, what else would it be, right?" He takes a moment to compose himself whilst Janos and I gather up the equipment – our denuded backpacks, some recording equipment, nothing special – and gingerly pack it into the middle of the boat. Then Janos climbs on board and holds a hand out for me. Usually this would get the old feminist hackles right up, but there's something charmingly old school about Janos. It seems that whatever former Eastern Block country he's from (he did tell me once, but it technically doesn't exist any more) manners are not dead.

It takes all of a minute for us to settle and Nik takes up the oars again. He swings to the right, avoiding the place, he got into trouble before – if it was a stray current (and who knows in this place? For all we know, nothing works as it should down here as no one's ever managed to find a substantial body of water this deep before) he's pretty keen to avoid it. I watch as the paddles dip into the dark water, causing ripples that undulate out, marking our passage from the shore when something else catches my eye.

"Hey… did you see that?"

Both Nik and Janos glance up at me, puzzled looks on their faces. Obviously not.

I peer back down, trying to penetrate the layers of blackness to see if I can catch a glimpse of it again, but there is nothing there. I thought I saw something pale glide by, nothing specific. Just a hint of a shadow of a possible shape, but it's gone. If it was ever there in the first place.

"Never mind," I say.

Nik keeps rowing. By now, the glow in the distance is more defined and I'm pretty sure I can make out the jagged outline of a rocky outcrop. Three slivers of light bob near its base – the rest of our team, or so I guess. Still we keep going, the sound of the oars splashing softly as Nik pulls them the only thing that breaks the silence.

I catch my breath when the inflatable skips, as if over a small collection of waves. Janos frowns, and Nik's eyes dart all over the place, nervously.

"Another current?" Janos asks.

Nik shrugs. "I guess so-"

His answer is cut off as something grazes the underside of the inflatable.

Nik's reaction is instantaneous. He draws the paddles in and freezes.

"What the hell was that?" I whisper, visions of amorphous pale things slithering through my head.

"Sand bar?" Janos says.

"Can you see a sand bar?" I say.

It's Janos' turn to shrug.

"I can't see m– whoa!'

The inflatable wheels around, as if someone had taken hold of the front and pushed it. I grab onto the little guide ropes that run its length and hang on tight. I didn't think it was possible, but Nik's gone even paler. Janos, on the other hand, is scanning the surface, looking for a culprit.

"Nik – row," he says. "Get out of here."

But Nik can't row. Nik's frozen, like me. We're both staring at each other, daring not to look over the water. The boat lifts again, and then without any warning, something huge erupts from the surface and slaps down hard. It is easily as big as the dinghy, and a mottled pale grey. Maybe I wasn't imagining things after all.

That galvanises Nik. Now he can't row fast enough. He isn't using the smooth, confident strokes of before – now he's jerking on the paddles wildly, stirring up the water, sending us in circles. Janos topples back and starts swearing in a language I don't understand (well, it sounds like swearing – if he isn't, his native tongue is the single most awesome language ever invented). It takes him a moment to find his feet before he wrenches one of the paddles from Nik's hand. He holds it in front of him, like a weapon, and I'm not sure if he means to help us get to safety or smack whatever it was that attacked the boat. Before I can make up my mind, I feel the rubber at my feet bulge upwards. I try to swallow, but my throat feels like it's made of sandpaper. I lift my foot, and the whole world turns upside down.

Quite literally.

A flash of orange is replaced by pitch-black so cold it stops my heart. Even the thick neoprene of my environment can't keep it out. It floods my mouth and tracks a burning trail to my lungs. It takes my mind a few seconds to realise what has happened. When it does, panic grips me. Which way is up? Down? I flail around, fighting down the urge to scream, fighting to find the surface. Something grabs at my arm. I struggle against it, but instead of letting go, it pulls me up. My head breaks the surface and I realise it is Janos. For once, his stoic mask has slipped – his dark eyes are huge, his mouth a rictus of fear. It's weird how you notice these little things when you're fighting for your life. It's like your brain decides its going to divert your attention to other things whilst it goes off and whimpers in the corner.

I try to take in a breath, but end up choking as the freezing fluid I have inhaled fights to be expelled. Janos has grabbed hold of what looks like a fragment of our inflatable; one of the ballast compartments, I think. The rest is in tatters around us. There are shouts from my left. Small pinpricks of light bob around, and I hear splashing.

"What the hell?"

"Are you guys all right?"

"What the fuck was that?"

The babble of questions brings me to my senses, just a little bit. It's enough for me to be gather myself; whatever hit the boat was moving, and that means I need to get out of the water. I flail my arms and legs around, trying to remember how to swim. Then I feel a strange pulling sensation, like I'm caught in a current. I glance around myself, but I can't see anything in the gloom.

"Swim!" Janos cries, and lets go of the remains of the dinghy.

I'm not a hugely good swimmer. I'm usually the queen of the slow breast stroke and that's about it, but I crawled away from that dinghy like an Olympian, following Janos towards the lights – and, I hoped, the shore. Behind me, the water explodes again and there's a deafening popping sound as the last of the air chambers in the inflatable gives way under… whatever it is. I can't think about it. I don't want to know. I just want to get away from it. I kick, frantic, scooping handfuls of water away from me until finally, my fingers scrape rock and I realise I'm able to stand up. I half-run, half-stagger into the shallows, where Marcus catches me.

"Fucking hell, Meg!" he says, his eyes like saucers. "What the hell happened?"

I can't answer him. I'm too busy bringing up mouthfuls of briny water and trying to breathe. Janos is doing the same.

"Where's Nik?" Fi asks.

I sway upright.

"He… he was… he… right behind?" Janos manages.

The urge to cough grips me again as sticky tendrils of dread clutch as my throat. No one speaks as we scan the water's edge.

Nik is nowhere to be seen.

Chapter Three

We called out over that ancient sea for what felt like hours, hoping that our cries would bring Nik back. But he never answered. He's gone. One by one, we abandoned our fruitless searching (if you call screaming someone's name over and over again whilst splashing about in the shallows of some god-forsaken underground sea 'searching') and sat on the cold rock of the headland. We didn't speak. I was freezing, but since there was no way to warm myself up, I didn't complain.

Someone sits next to me, heavily. It's Janos. He looks haunted. I shake my head and dare to pat him on the back. I know how he feels, but it isn't his fault.

Fi soon joins us, followed by Brendan and then Marcus. We avoid looking at each other; avoid speaking, even though I know we're all thinking the same thing.

What the fuck just happened?

Brendan breaks the silence.

"What was it?"

"What was what?" I reply, wearily.

"What… what did that?"

"I dunno. You're supposed to be the cave ecologist. You tell me."

When he doesn't answer, Fi takes up the slack

"What happened?" she asks, her voice low.

I grind my teeth together. What what what what what. Fuck off. Like I know.

"Something came up underneath us," Janos says. "Something big."

"Something alive?"

Janos just shrugs and glances to me. No point looking this way, big guy. I have no idea what it was either.

"So, we're facing the very real possibility that there's something large and quite possibly carnivorous living down there?" Marcus says after a long pause. "Great."

"I don't know." I say. For some reason, Marcus's attitude is making me feel angry. "No one really saw anything. For all we know, it could have been a… a rogue current, or an unforeseen outcrop of rock just below the surface." Which has the ability to leap out of the water and chomp boats to bits.

"Oh yeah? Then where's Nik? And while we're at it, where's the fucking boat?" Marcus stands up, his hands on his head. He spins on the spot. "We're three fucking miles down, with no equipment and no way of letting those above know things have gone to shit-"

"Sit down, Marcus," Fi says.

"I will not sit down!" Marcus snaps back. His hands come off his head and he starts throwing them around like a crazy person trying to direct imaginary traffic. "Hasn't it occurred to you? Is this what happened to the Alpha Team? They tried to cross that damn lake and… it got them."

"It?"

"Whatever is living in the fucking water!"

"We don't know if there is an 'it' yet."

"It is an 'it'," says Janos. His gaze slides from the water and settles on Fi. "Megan saw it first. Nik thought it was, you know, reflections in the water playing mind-tricks, but then something hit the boat. It knew we were coming. It knew what to do."

"Oh, this gets better and better!" Marcus says.

"Brendan?" Fi says.

"What?"

"Like Meg said, you're the expert. What do you think?"

Brendan looks back over the water, chewing on the side of his thumb. "I don't know-"

"Oh, great – if you don't know, why did you even bother coming?" Marcus starts.

"I don't know because this whole scenario is new," Brendan cuts in. "Not just new to me, but new in general. Underground seas are usually accessed by bore holes. You don't tend to just stumble on them like we did. So no, I don't have a clue what it might have been. And, to bę honest, I wouldn't like to speculate."

"Rather than worrying about whether we can identify the inhabitants of the lake, maybe we should be thinking about finding ways back to the main shore?" Janos says.

"Oh yeah," Marcus says. "We'll just go and lop a few palm trees down and lash the logs together with vines – that should make a nice raft. Oh, no, wait a moment. We can't do that because there aren't any fucking trees down here – or indeed anything that fucking floats!"

"Marcus," I say. "Calm down." His theatrics are starting to give me a migraine, and the last thing I need is one of those, especially since my migraine meds are at the bottom of this godforsaken sea right now. He goes to snap at me, but I pull my best 'teacher says shut the fuck up' face and he rocks back a bit. I don't use it often, but it shuts up arrogant undergrads, so why not him too?

"Best thing to do," Fi says, trying to sound confident and assertive, "is have a look around here. See where we are. Have a look at what provisions we do have. Try to come up with some kind of strategy. Remember, once they realise they've lost contact with us as well, they'll realise we're in trouble and need help."

"Or decide this whole endeavour was a ridiculous waste of time and forget about us," Marcus grumbles under his breath. This time, both Janos and I shoot him stony looks. Fi carries on.

"They sent help after the Alpha Team. They'll send help after us. Nobody gets left behind."

Nobody gets left behind. Heh. I'm surprised Marcus didn't kick off again at that one. That's a military platitude, one Fi learned during her time with the US Marines. She's a good lass – I can't really call her a 'girl' since she'd probably punch me into next week if I did – with a good heart, but her military training means she tends to see things in the simplest of ways. What she tends to forget is this is not a military endeavour. I know, and judging by the looks the others are giving each other, they do too, that if a rescue mission is considered too risky (or, God forbid, too expensive), then they will leave us down here to rot.

"Hang on... what's that?" Brendan says, breaking through my morbid train of thought. I look up and follow his line of sight.

Something pale is floating in the shallows.

We all inch to our feet. It's bobbing in the slight current, a formless mass. My stomach sinks. I'm not running over there, and it seems like I'm not the only one having reservations. I know what it might be, and I'm not sure I'm ready to face the consequences of that right now. We've been sat here bickering for what? Half an hour? An hour? There's no way he would survive being underwater that long.

"Oh, for Christ's sake, I'll go." Fi says. In a fit of bravado, she stomps through the shallows, sending up graceful fans of frigid water with every step. My heart jolts into my throat. For some reason, on a deep, instinctual level, I know that's a bad idea.

Fi approaches the mass and stoops down to investigate it. My hand flies involuntarily to my mouth as I bite down on the urge to scream at her, to tell her to get the hell out of the water. Instead, I hold my breath and dare not move.

"Fucking hell..." she says as she hauls the pale thing out of the water. "Would you come and have a look at this?"

By an unspoken agreement of glances and tiny shrugs, Janos strides in after her. They have a brief conversation that I can't quite make out before he grabs part of the... whatever it is Fi has found, and together they drag it back to shore.

I'm not sure if I'm happy or disappointed it's not Nik. If he had drowned, then maybe we could have kept fooling ourselves that what happened was down to rogue currents and a horrible accident.

What Fi and Janos bring back is far more horrifying.

The remains of the inflatable dinghy are in tatters. Ragged ends of yellow rubber waft like entrails in the slight current. Fi lifts up a section of it and inspects it closely.

"It looks as if it has been mauled by something."

Considering the dinghy could comfortably seat four people, we don't have to say what we're all thinking. A quick glance suffices. Whatever the 'something' was, in order to do this much damage, it must have been pretty big.

"So..." says Marcus to Brendan. "Come on, expert. What do you reckon?"

Brendan gazes over the now-calm water, his eyes narrowed, as if trying to spot the culprit. “Like I said before, I don’t know.”

“Well, whatever it was, it left something behind,” Fi says. We all turn to watch her as she pries something out of the rubber. It’s embedded in one of the plastic paddle-mounts, but she eventually manages to lever it out with the tip of her knife.

“Jesus…” she breathes as she weighs in it the palm of her hand. “Look at the size of that…”

A tooth. But not just any old tooth. This one is about five inches long, conical, with regular striations along its length. It is pointed, vicious. At one end, pink gum still gleams wetly.

“What the fuck is that from?” Marcus asks. “A shark?”

I shake my head. I’ve found enough shark teeth in my time to know what they look like.

“No. Shark teeth are invariably triangular, with serrated edges.” I beckon to Fi, wordlessly asking if I can hold her prize. She hands it over and then unconsciously wipes her hands down her thighs, as if that might wipe away all contact with the things that caused Nik’s demise.

“It’s heavy. This thing is used to tearing into things – things that struggle.”

Like me.

I’m struggling. I’m struggling because I have seen a tooth like this before. Three years previous, Oxford Clay, Peterborough, England. Embedded in a jaw fragment. Not as big as this, but almost identical in morphology.

“Pliosaur,” Janos says quietly.

I jerk my head up. Is he reading my thoughts? His dark eyes are wide and never leave the tooth in my hand.

I nod. “That’s my thoughts too.”

“Plio-what?” Marcus asks.

“Pliosaur,” I say. I feel oddly detached from myself, as if I’m actually standing a couple of feet away, watching myself speak. “Jurassic marine predator. Nine known genera, I think, with the largest being discovered in Svalbard, although experts think the one unearthed in Dorset might be even bigger.” I swallow. “They call the Svarlbard one 'Predator X' and reckon that bastard could’ve reached sizes of up to fifty feet in length.”

Marcus snorts derisively, but Janos nods at everything I say.

"Ambush predator," he adds, "was known for its unique method of locomotion – only the related plesiosaurs swam in a similar way - and their huge, tooth-filled skulls."

I give Janos an enquiring look.

"Yeah, you're right. How do you know that?"

He shrugs. "Don't all small boys like dinosaurs at some point?" He flashes me a blink-and-you'd-miss-it smile before looking serious again. "But they all died out by the end of the Cretaceous. Changing environments, competition, salinity… they died out before the K/T extinction. This cannot be."

I test the weight of the tooth in my hand. He's right, of course – there's no way it could be true. Absolute nonsense to even entertain the notion. But the tooth is here. Here, in my hand. Exactly the same as the Liopleurodon tooth found in the Oxford Clay in Peterborough, only an inch and a half bigger.

"So… what you're saying is there's a huge fuck-off monster that should have died out what… seventy million years ago? But despite that, it's in these waters and it possibly just ate Nik?" The brutality of Marcus's tight statement makes me wince. Just ate Nik. No attempt at sugar coating it, just bald reality. Or surrealism. Or whatever passes for reality here. I don't know any more. "Bullshit," Marcus says. "This is all bullshit."

"This system has been isolated from the surface since the Jurassic period," Brendan says. He's looking thoughtful, and nods to me, his hand outstretched. I pass him the tooth, careful not to touch the flesh still clinging to it. For some reason, that freaks me out. The tooth on its own? I could pretend its nothing more than a fossil, a relic from a time long gone. But the flesh… the flesh tells another story. It's fresh. It's real. And it's here.

"And?" Marcus says.

"Could be a case of convergent evolution," Brendan says. "Something fitting into a niche within an environment causing them to take on a familiar form. There are creatures we call spiders living in caves that have nothing to do with the arachnid family – they've just evolved that form because it serves the environment the animal lives in the best way."

I find myself nodding. "Yeah, like ichthyosaurs and dolphins," I say. "They look really similar, exploited similar environmental riches, but were two totally disparate species – one's a reptile, the other a mammal."

"So… what?" asks Fi. "You're saying whatever is in there isn't a relic from prehistoric times?"

"Well… no," says Brendan, looking awkward. "I'm no expert, but that's one possible explanation. The other is that this environment was somehow protected and whilst other species died out, this one survived and has been evolving down here, apart from the rest of the natural world. It happens. Look at the Coelacanth. Thought extinct for 65 million years, then in 1938, one turns up in a fish market in Africa."

"Yeah, but that's just a fish."

"A pretty big fish. I mean, big enough for the world to take notice."

"Yeah, but it wasn't a fifty foot fucking monster, was it?" Marcus explodes. "Would you all listen to yourselves? You all sound like nutcases! Jurassic marine predators surviving to modern times… it's like some shitty sci-fi movie they show at 3am because by then you're too shitfaced to care about logic!"

"Okay, fine - then what do you think attacked the boat, Marcus?" Brendan asks. "And what about this?" He brandishes the tooth like the Sword of Truth.

"Fuck that!" Before any of us can stop him, Marcus lunges forwards and grabs the tooth out of Brendan's hand. He winds his arm back and throws. The tooth spins end over end before plopping into the waters of the ancient lake.

"What the… what the hell did you do that for?" I feel rage, real, red hot rage well up within me. I'm usually pretty easy going if I do say so myself, but watching that ignorant prick hurl something so precious, so… so… *unique* out into the depths just because he isn't ready to face the reality of our situation makes my blood boil. I clench my fist to stop myself from slapping him. "That was the only hard evidence of what might be living out there."

"Boo fucking hoo," Marcus mutters.

That's it. I've had enough of him. Arrogant wanker, always trying it on, disguising his misogyny as playful banter. I take a step forward, but before I can raise a hand, I feel a gentle pressure upon my shoulder. I whip around, ready to confront whoever dares to try to stop me from sorting the arrogant little prick out, and I am faced with Janos, a small crease of concern between his eyes, shaking his head.

"What is done is done," he says. "It is not worth it. We need to focus on what is important."

"But he-"

"Yes, I know. But it doesn't matter. Not now. Now, we need to work out what to do next. That is what matters."

His voice, with that heavy almost Russian lilt of his, is quite hypnotic.

I take in a deep breath to quell the fire inside me. He's right. What's proof of any kind if no one gets to see it?

Marcus sneers at Janos, but is sensible enough not to say anything. Janos might be our gentle giant, but even he has limits, and this place is enough to push anyone to the very limit of theirs.

"So… what now?" Brendan asks, tentatively.

"I guess… I guess we have a look around," says Fi. "Find out what's here. Establish some kind of camp. See if there might be another way back to the main shore."

Whilst I agree with everything she's saying, I can't help my attention from being diverted. A weird crackling sound on the edge of my hearing bugs me. It sputters in fits and starts, like a fly banging against a windowpane.

"If there is, then it might be sensible to – I'm sorry, Megan, am I boring you?" Fi sounds testy, so I drag my attention back.

"No, sorry, not at all. But… can't you hear that?"

They all fall silent for a moment, and there it is again, a weird, buzzing noise. Like… static?

"Fuck, that's the radio!" Brendan says. He leaps forward, towards the water, yelling. "Hey! HEY! WE'RE HERE! We can't get out! HELP!"

The water in front of him boils, as if something has just flipped over just below the surface. He steps back, away from the shallows.

"They won't be able to hear you," Marcus says. "Retard."

"Don't call him a retard," I snap. Marcus is really getting on my tits now. I will quite happily lamp him one if he doesn't shut the hell up sometime soon.

"He has a point," Fi says. "You need someone to press the button to reply, remember?"

So close, yet so far. The other shore only has to be – what – fifty? Seventy five feet away? If it were a swimming pool, none of us would baulk. But it's not a swimming pool. It's a black stretch of freezing water of indeterminate depth with… something living in it.

Something big.

Something that, despite us being on land, hasn't moved away in search of food elsewhere

"Fuck," Brendan mutters. I can't help but agree with him. Fuck indeed.

Chapter Four

I really need a cigarette. I gave up smoking eight years ago, but right now, I'd give my left tit for a ciggie. Fuck it, I'd let Marcus cop a feel of my left tit if he had one I could spark up. But he doesn't, so I won't. Good job, really. Not a good place to be prostituting yourself for a cigarette.

We still haven't found any evidence of the Alpha Team. God knows what happened to them. It's this, on top of everything else, that's really strung everyone out.

What happened to Team Alpha?

It hangs over us like a bad smell. No one has said it. No one needs to. But, by some unspoken agreement, we all peer behind every boulder, glance up at every nook, investigate every cranny, just in case there's something, anything, there that gives us a hint.

The cove that we landed in is really small. It took us a good half hour to get everyone up the cliff side – it's not so much that it's steep, but more dark and everyone's on edge. Once we're up, we get a better view of what we're dealing with.

Apart from the small stretch of beach that we came from, all we can see is water.

It's weird. I can't describe it. It's like looking out over the ocean at night, but there's no horizon; no stars; no clouds. Just water and blackness. For a moment, I feel like I'm floating, suspended above the blackness with nothing but rippling light as my companion. Then I hear a splash, and I'm brought back down to earth.

"Would you look at that," Fi breathes beside me.

Just on the edge of our torch light, a huge hump breaks the surface. It's too dim to make out any details. It looks like a massive, smooth boulder has just breached and then sunk back down beneath the rippling surface.

"Well, I think that confirms it breathes air," Brendan says. "Means it still could be some kind of whale..."

"Still could be some kind of pliosaur," Janos says.

We all glance away. Everyone apart from Marcus, who just stares at Janos like he's some kind of mad man. No one wants to admit that whatever it is might be the relic from some ancient past, because admitting that kind of puts you somewhere on a par with people who think they've been abducted by aliens and that Essex is crawling with lions, but Marcus seems to take Janos's rather flippant comment way too personally.

"Would you shut the hell up about fucking pliosaurs," he says, his teeth gritted, his lips a thin line. "It's not a fucking pliosaur – in order for it to be a fucking pliosaur, there would need to be a surviving population down here – one that's managed to sustain its numbers over a hundred million years. And whilst I am not doubting that sea is vast, it isn't that fucking vast. So Shut. Up."

"And you think a whale is more of a viable option?" Janos counters. "How do you think it got down here? Washed down with the rain? We are three miles underground. Whatever it is, it has evolved down here. That there is anything huge at all in the water is a goddamned miracle."

"He's right," Brendan says. "Whatever that thing is, there will be a sustained breeding population, which means it evolved down here. It is a goddamned miracle. Some cave fish get pretty big, but nothing like this. So, in a way, it doesn't matter if it is a whale or some kind of ancient marine reptile or something no one has ever even thought of before – the bottom line is, it shouldn't be here. But it is."

"And it's hunting us," I whisper.

Now it's their turn to stare at me. I have no idea why I said that out loud. It's been something that's been playing on my mind for a while.

Why is it still here? Why won't it leave?

Because of us.

Because it's eaten humans before, and it knows we're easy prey.

"Bullshit," Marcus says. "By your own logic, that's a crock. If it's been down here for 200 millions years plus, then it hasn't come across humans before."

"Apart from the other team." I say. Inside my head, I'm railing at myself – shut up! I can't believe you just said that! And judging by Fi's sharp intake of breath, I have just dared to speak the unspeakable. But I'm right. I know I am. Otherwise, where are they?

I can tell Marcus is torn, because he doesn't jump down my throat. Instead, he stares moodily over the water, biting the edge of his thumb.

"Whatever," Fi says, breaking the silence. "It doesn't matter. We still have the rest of this… whatever it is to explore. You never know, there might be a way back that doesn't involve swimming."

Even I, with my meagre experience and knowledge of caves, can tell she's clutching at straws.

* * *

We spend about an hour following the coast. It's not really a coast, but we don't really know what else to call it, so that'll have to do. With each step it's becoming clearer that this is some kind of island, a huge outcrop of rock that stands guard to what I keep persisting to think of as a harbour, like a mini Isle of Wight, minus the tourists and ice cream.

In a strange way, I'm grateful for the glow of the bacteria. I have no idea what genus it is, and the light it sheds (if you can call it that) doesn't really illuminate as much as enhance the shadows, but at least it means it isn't pitch black down here. Every now and again, I hear the rippling of water as the thing surfaces, but none of us catches sight of it again. Still, I can't shake off the feeling it's watching us, waiting.

Once we establish that this is indeed an island, we move inland. There are no plants here, not even algae. Once you get away from the water's edge, the rock is as dry and bare as bone. It makes sense. There is no sunlight, so how could anything survive? By the water, though, it's a different matter. As well as the ever-present glowing bacteria, there are clumps of huge molluscs that resemble malformed mussels, and thin fronds of some kind of algae extend from the rocks to create a strange parody of seaweed. Brendan even spies little crabs scuttling around, and Janos pointed out a primitive-looking fish to me, no longer than my finger and as pale as a ghost. Once I get my eye in, there's more to be found – spiky black echinoderms crawl through forests of blobby anenomes, which in turn are accompanied by the weirdest looking shrimps – all feelers and claws – I've ever seen. For so long we've lived under the illusion that there's nothing but mineral beneath our feet, but this place proves that once life is established, it will find a way. All of a sudden, all those mad books about a Hollow Earth and Jules Verne's idea of an ecosystem at the centre of the planet don't seem quite so far-fetched. I feel humbled and a little frightened in the face of it all. We think we're so important, that we are the keepers of the keys, but in reality, we're nothing more than children stumbling around in the dark, flicking switches and trampling on ants' nests just to see what might happen.

Fi's leading us now. Funny, since Nik disappeared, no one has really mentioned him, even though he was kind of our unspoken leader. Out of all of us, he'd had by far the most experience in dealing with new cave systems and his cautious manner meant it felt only natural for him to take the lead. I'd always thought his second in command was Janos, but he seems reluctant to step up and fill the vacant role. Instead, he spends most of his time skulking at the back. So Fi stepped up. I'm glad she did. Her military background means she's efficient, if a little brusque, and best of all, she doesn't take any of Marcus's shit.

Marcus. Now there's one who goes to show you don't really know someone until you're stranded three miles underground on an ancient island whilst something predatory may or may not be circling it in the water, waiting for you to go for a paddle. He's always been a bit of a prick, but I'd put him down as one of those Marmite people – you know, you either love him or hate him, but he's effectively harmless. Now I know he's anything but harmless. In fact, I would say he's downright dangerous.

"What the hell are we playing at?" he says for about the seventeenth time. "We need to get off the island, not go further into it."

I hear Fi sigh, but she says nothing. It's Brendan who tries to placate him this time, telling him we're just having a look, that look, which we need to know exactly what we're up against so we can make an informed decision as what to do next-

That's about as far as he got before Marcus blows up again, swearing, calling us all stupid fuckers, what the fuck are we playing at, there's no point to this, we're just making busy work in an attempt at not facing up to reality and accepting that we are well and truly screwed.

And you know what? If he wasn't being a total asshole about it all, I'd probably be agreeing with him. But just as wandering around this lump of rock is futile, so is screaming about it. So I shut up, grit my teeth and press on.

***

"Holy shit…"

As usual, Fi's up ahead. We've been clambering up the side of a rock face for a good quarter of an hour. It's not high, just difficult. The limestone has given way to a patch of fissile shale, making climbing a treacherous joy. Climbers don't usually bother with shale. It's too much like hard work, and you're just as likely to come away with a handful of rock dust and splinters as a firm handhold, but we don't have much of a choice. Either we get over this, or we head back. And no-one feels like heading back, because there's nothing to head back to.

It isn't the shale that caused Fi to swear, though. Both Brendan and Marcus are caught short when they reach the top – Janos had to catch Brendan's heel before he toppled backwards – but once I'm up there, I can see why.

I'm not sure how to begin describing it, but it isn't natural, that's one thing I am sure of.

I can't exactly say how big it is due to the quality (or lack of quality) of the light. But standing here, I guess it's easily a hundred feet tall, if not more. A perfectly circular column, constructed from a gleaming pale rock. At least I think it's rock. Maybe. The closer we get, the less sure I am.

"What the fuck is that?" Marcus breathes, all former irritation at our predicament lost.

I can't answer him. My mouth is dry, and my tongue feels about five sizes too big. Instead, I shake my head and shrug.

"Some kind of crystal?" Brendan asks.

Again, all I can do is shrug. It's like nothing I've ever seen before. I get the sneaking suspicion it's unlike anything anyone has seen before.

We approach slowly, as if the column is somehow going to wake up and swallow us whole. And in a weird way, it does. As we creep closer, I notice a dark splodge at its base. I pause, squinting, but my eyes stubbornly refuse to focus. I go to mention this to the others, but they have all continued on.

"Hey, wait up," I say. Fi gives me one of those half-quizzical, half annoyed looks that parents often give their kids when they know they should be paying attention to what their darlings are doing, but aren't really all that interested. I realise that her attitude just about sums up my place here. I'm not a survivalist, not a caver - I'm just a stupid rock-monkey in her eyes, the drummer of the scientific world, brought a long way because the oil company insisted. Anger prickles at me. If they're all so experienced, then why haven't they noticed the splodge?

"I said, hang on." I quickstep up to them, forcing my way next to Fi, determined to make her listen to me.

"What is it?" Her tone is clipped, which raises my hackles even further.

"Since none of you experts have mentioned it – anyone else notice anything odd about that column?" I'm sorry, but I'm not handing it to her on a plate.

"What, apart from the fact that it's fucking weird?" Marcus says from behind us.

"No… look closer. Near the base."

We peer into the gloom. It's Fi's turn to shrug.

"A patch of shadow? Nothing usual about that, Meg – the light's not exactly great here."

"I think it's an opening."

There. I've said it.

"She's right," Janos says, after a heavy pause. "Now I look at it carefully, it seems too regular to be just a patch of shadow."

"An opening? Like a crack?" Brendan says.

"Of course it's a crack," Marcus says. "What else would it be? A door?" He lets out a bark of laughter, and I suddenly feel foolish. Why did I let my stupid prideful paranoia get in the way? I should have just shut up, put up and let them discover it themselves.

Whatever it is.

"Well, opening or not, standing here isn't getting us anywhere," Fi says, like a true leader. Again. It's beginning to wind me up a little bit, actually. Can't hang around here. Standing here won't get us anywhere. We need to move out. Listen to me, I know best. That's all she knows. That's all she understands-

Wait a minute. Just... wait a sec. Where is all of this coming from? For some reason, what was once just a mild annoyance is now something I'd quite like to hurt people over. Which is ridiculous. I spare Marcus a glance. He's muttering under his breath, his mouth moving like he's got something stuck in his teeth. Maybe his sudden change in demeanour is understandable. Maybe it isn't him at all.

Maybe it's this place.

They talk about cabin fever, and deep sea narcosis – maybe this is the caving equivalent? We're three miles down, after all; who knows how the physical stresses we're under might affect us? And that's without everything that has happened to us. A shiver trickles down my spine, and the desire to get away from this place hits hard. I look back to the column, and the feeling intensifies. It's perfectly round and perfectly straight, apart from the patch of darkness at its base. If it's a natural formation, it's like nothing I've ever seen or heard of before. We creep closer.

"That isn't right," Janos says, and I can only agree with him. Marcus and Brendan stop. Even Fi takes a step back.

I was reluctant to say what I thought the splodge was before, just in case I was wrong. Because things like that shouldn't exist three miles under the surface of the Earth, in a cave that has been cut off from the surface for around a hundred and sixty million years. But we're close enough now to see the truth, and there's no denying it.

It's a door.

Not a door in the sense of a front door, but a definite cut in the surface of the column that is covered by a darker material. It has shapes carved into it. Actual shapes, like you might find in an ancient tomb or something.

"All right. Okay. What the fuck?" Marcus says. "I thought this cave had only just been discovered? As in, 'untouched by human hands'? Then why is there a fucking inscribed door down here?"

None of us can answer his rather eloquently put question, because none of us have a clue.

"Maybe it's… it's an artefact, or something," Fi says. "You know, a natural formation that just happens to look like it was created by someth… one."

I can't help but notice the correction, and the way the others look at her. Scary thing is, I think what she was going to say is more accurate. Something, not someone.

Some*thing*.

To my surprise, Brendan is the first to approach the door. I always put him down as a bit of a natural, well, not a coward, but definitely more cautious than the likes of Fi or Marcus. Now, roles are reversed. The adrenaline junkies, those seekers of the ultimate highs, are hanging back, their eyes goggling, their hands shaking as Brendan reaches up to touch the darker stone of the door. My breath catches in my throat, curtailing any attempt at telling him not to. He pauses, his fingertips just hovering over its surface. I jump when something touches my lips, and feel foolish when I realise it's my own hand.

"It doesn't look natural to me," Brendan whispers. He turns. "Meg?"

All eyes are on me. In a way, this is why I am here. I'm the geologist, after all.

I wander over on legs made of elastic to stand beside him. He's breathing hard, and little droplets of sweat stand from his brow. He's afraid, and he has every right to be, because when you're this close, it's plain the door isn't natural.

Sometimes, nature mimics humanity. For years, a bunch of scratches on a rock in Norway was thought to be one of the earliest forms of runic writing. People spent years trying to decipher them, to work out what our ancient ancestors thought so important that it had to be written down. That is, until someone realised they were just scratches all along.

There's no mistaking this. Nature may mimic humanity in many ways, but it doesn't draw perfectly symmetrical designs into an iron-hard rock I can't identify.

"Who built it?" Brendan murmurs.

"I don't know," I say. "I'm not an archaeologist. They didn't think we'd need one down here." I spare him a look before my attention is dragged back to the swirling designs. "I guess they were wrong."

"That's one way of putting it."

His hand is hovering just above the door's surface. I hear him swallow. Then, before I can stop him, he touches it.

As soon as his fingertips touch the rock, my ears pop. Brendan freezes for a split second, his fingers all but fused to the door, and then drops his hand. He blinks.

"What was that?"

The question makes us both jump.

"Dunno," Brendan says, turning around. The others are crowded around us, each face a picture of concern.

"Felt like a… a… drop in pressure, or something," I say.

"Yeah," Fi says, and scratches her nose.

"Uh, guys…" Marcus says. "Where's the door?"

What does he mean, where's the door? I look around, back to where Brendan touched the stone… but Marcus is right. It's not there any more. Instead, a gaping black hole stands.

A way in.

"Did… anyone hear anything move?" Marcus asks. We all shake our heads. My mouth feels sticky and I'm finding it hard to swallow.

Whatever is going on here has just got about a hundred times weirder.

Marcus steps up and inspects the portal. He's frowning, and I don't blame him.

"There's nothing. Nothing at all." He runs a hand over his buzz cut. "Jesus, man – what's going on here? Doors just don't fucking disappear like that!"

"Heh, why not? Considering we shouldn't be finding doors in places where humans have never been," Brendan says.

We all stare at him. He has said the unspeakable.

"Oh, come on, guys! We're all thinking it. It's about time we admitted it. This isn't right. It's an established fact that the last time this cave complex was connected with the surface was during the Cretaceous at the very latest, so why are there doors down here? This is clearly something constructed… so who built it? It can't be humankind… and so what's left?"

"No – don't be stupid-" Fi starts.

"Why is it stupid, Fi" Brendan continues. There's a fire in his voice now, and it scares me a bit. Who knew? Looks like Brendan might be one of those 'was God an astronaut' types.

Great.

"Because I'm not thinking what you're thinking," Fi says, slowly. "I'm thinking we're all really tired and more than likely traumatised by what happened to Nik. I think we need to take a step back and start being sensible-"

"Sensible? Oh, come off it! It's right in front of us, Fi. How can you deny it? For God's sake, look! There was a door here – one covered in carvings and patterns – and now there isn't. I touched it and it opened. You all saw it."

"Look, we don't know what we saw," Fi says. "This place is unique, with a potential set of unique conditions in which it formed. The... the 'door' could have just been... just been come kind of special, uh, cooling formation, or, or..."

It's clear to me that she is struggling to try to rationalise what's happening to us. Brendan, on the other hand, just gets angry.

"What?" Brendan's frustration is plain now. If this were a cartoon, there would be steam shooting out of his ears. "But that's not true, is it? You saw it. We all saw it. We all saw the door. The carvings. Before I touched it. Didn't we?" He turns to me, looking for confirmation. "Meg?"

Oh, crap. My stomach plummets. Not fair, Brendan – not fair. I have no desire to get mixed up in this, no desire whatsoever. Looks like I don't have a choice, though.

I close my eyes, resigning myself to my fate, and nod. I can feel Fi's disapproval and Brendan's triumph like ice and fire against my skin.

"See? I told you. It was here."

Yes, so he's right. Oh, but how I wish he wasn't. Now it's Brendan's turn to sound like a lunatic. I wonder when it will be mine.

"Megan, you're the rock expert. Were they carvings? They weren't just… I don't know, some kind of weird natural formation in the rock?"

Now my hackles rise. My eyes fly open, and I fix Fi with my hardest stare. There she goes again, doubting me, deriding me. As if I wouldn't be able to tell the difference between natural phenomena and full on cave art. Bitch. Then the memory of the deluded Norwegians and their Viking runes floats to the surface. They were experts, too, and just as sure. But they were wrong. Maybe I'm wrong. Maybe I was just looking for patterns in the chaos.

Or maybe my mind is giving me the excuse I need so I don't have to face up to the reality that maybe, just maybe, the nutters are right and we are not alone.

I shrug. It's a good response. Nothing says, "I don't know and please, don't push it" like a shrug. Fi accepts it with a sage nod of her head, but Brendan isn't having any of it.

"Megan? Please! Why are you… why deny it? You saw it! We all saw it"

"I did," I say eventually. "But, Brendan – I don't know what it was. It's so dark down here, and like Fi says, we're tired and stressed and-"

"And what? I can't believe that you're denying the evidence of your own eyes!"

Why is he picking on me? Why doesn't he drag the other two into this? They saw it too, after all. I know what Fi's doing, and I don't blame her. I don't blame her, because doors shouldn't exist down here, even if you have seen one with your own eyes-

"Maybe if we enter, we could settle this once and for all?"

There goes Janos again, being all reasonable. Well, maybe not reasonable, considering what he is suggesting – whether I was wrong about the pictures on a door that doesn't seem to exist any more or not, I'm not going in there, not unless I have to – but at least he's not arguing. Brendan snaps his head up, as if he'd forgotten Janos was even there, and his eyes brighten. He nods enthusiastically. I wonder what's happened to the cautious, sweet nerdy bloke I met three weeks ago, but he's gone, replaced by a doppelgänger I know only too well. Most scientists have one. It's the curse of curiosity. We want to know more, and sometimes, it makes us forget our fears and reservations. Sometimes it's a good thing; it's what drives us to answer seemingly impossible questions about life, the universe and everything, but sometimes it can get you into serious trouble. Like now.

"I don't know, Janos..." Fi says. She looks uneasy. Despite my previous feelings, I can't help but feel that she's the one we should be listening to right now. Good, solid, sensible Fi. Soldier Fi.

"Oh, come on, Lieutenant – aren't you just a little bit curious?" Marcus says. Fi and I exchange a look, aware that not only are we outnumbered, but also how this is turning into some kind of strange battle of the sexes, a playground-like mentality of boys vs girls. In the end, it is Fi who utilises the all-round shrug, and I am forced to join in. But I don't like it, and no one can make me.

Chapter Five

Although Brendan wants to go first, Fi won't let him. I don't blame her. He's turned into some kind of human/Labrador puppy hybrid, and his enthusiasm isn't so much catching as potentially deadly. He wants to bound into the darkness when we haven't a clue what's in there. I mean, we don't even know if there's a floor.

She spends a moment just looking at the doorway, and then with a determined grimace, pulls out her pick. She tests its weight as I imagine a warrior of old might do a sword and gives a grim nod.

She steps into the gloom and disappears.

Brendan makes to go next, but Janos stops him. A look is exchanged, and Janos wins out. He goes first, followed closely by Brendan. Marcus glances to me and gestures towards the doorway.

"Ladies first?"

Fuck you, Marcus. Fuck. You.

***

I don't know what I was expecting. How could I know? No one's ever been in this situation before. Oh, sure, people have wandered into undiscovered places before and marvelled at the wonderful sights that lay before them, but each time, they have been safe in the knowledge that everything they're about to discover was built by human hands, within the acceptable parameters of human experience.

We're not.

Beyond the door, it is dark. There aren't any bacteria in here, so it's pitch black. The light from our kinetic headlamps feels weak in here, their beams barely able to penetrate a blackness so thick it feels like this whole place is screaming, "get out whilst you still can!"

But we don't listen. We press on.

The column is hollow. Which makes it a tower, I suppose. Thinking of it as a tower makes my head ache, though, because we're back to that whole "calling it a tower gives it an air of being constructed and as far as I know, the dinosaurs didn't go in for much building" thing. But what else can we call it? There is literally nothing in my lexicon, both everyday and professional, that even begins to describe what this is. And judging by the way the others are turning slow circles, their faces slack, their eyes huge, they are struggling too. In a way, it's comforting to see them rattled. We're all in this together. That's something, at least.

Once our eyes adjust, we can see that the 'room' is only ten feet in diameter, but it soars above us, straight up, as far as we can see. The walls are made of the same strange, pale crystalline mineral as the outside. On the walls are images. It's like a graffiti artist decided to go on a massive trip and paint all the funny patterns he saw in huge, bold strokes. They look vaguely geometrical, but I can't work any of it out. I don't think anyone alive today could.

"Would you look at this shit…" Marcus breathes. "What does it mean?"

None of us answers him. It feels churlish to even try.

Janos steps further into the room and lets out a short, panicked bark. We all jump and go towards him, but he holds a shaking hand up and yells at us all to stop. Then he crouches down and runs his hand along the floor. By the light of his headlamp, I can now see why.

There's a hole in the floor, about three feet wide. Just big enough for someone to fall in and never be seen again.

We all join him at the edge and peer down. If we thought it was black up here, it's nothing compared to down there. Down there, it's as dark as the devil's arsehole and I for one am not all that keen on investigating further. There's something about the hole that makes me nervous, something beyond it just being dark and potentially deep. Little sparks of static panic ignite along my spine when I see Fi and Janos unholstering the two remaining coils of rope that we have.

"You're not… you're not thinking about going down there, are you?" I ask… It's hard to keep the tremble out of my voice, and I'm ashamed to admit my throat lumps up as tears back up behind my eyes. I swallow hard. What the hell is wrong with me? Like tears will stop them going down there.

Janos looks up and reaches out to pat my shoulder.

"We have to," he says. "We need to explore all avenues. You never know – this might help us find a way back."

Find a way back? Is he mad? Of course, this won't help us find a way back. I catch a glimpse of Marcus shaking his head in terrified disbelief. Brendan, on the other hand, cranes his neck so he can get a better look, his expression almost hungry.

He's really beginning to worry me.

After splicing their ropes with a complicated selection of knots, Fi tries to drive a spike into the lip of the hole. It doesn't even scratch the surface, let alone bite. She gives us all a look that borders on the apologetic.

"Sorry, had to try. Looks like we're going to have to fix this elsewhere."

We scour the room, looking for anything that we might use as an anchor point. After a few minutes, Marcus lets out a short, "Hey, guys," and we all crowd round him. What he's found makes my throat constrict.

On the wall, about four feet off the ground, is a metal ring. I say 'metal' because I can't figure out what it's made of and it's kind of shiny. It also doesn't have any discernible way of fixing it to the wall.

"Why… what? A ring? Why?" Fi asks, as perturbed as I am.

"You've gotta tie your guard dog to something," Marcus says. At first, I think he's joking, but a quick glance tells me that's not the case. He's serious. I eye the ring again. It's directly opposite the door.

Guard dog, indeed.

Janos gives it a tug.

"Well, whatever it is and why it is here, it is fortunate. It seems strong enough. We can use it."

I watch as Janos and Fi set up the ropes, the black sludge of doubt sloshing around my insides. I've done some pretty stupid things in my time, but this is definitely going to go down and a new contender for first place. We're rappelling down, so Janos goes first. He's pretty adamant about it, saying he set up the ropes and therefore should be the one to test them, which is one hundred percent fine by me. Every time I peer down that hole, I can't help but feel we're mucking around with things that should be left well alone.

After Janos goes Brendan, more because we can't stop him than out of any discernible choice. Then Marcus.

Then me.

Fi clips me onto the ropes and tries to give me a reassuring grin.

It doesn't work.

"You've had lots of practice at this," she says. "Just don't think about where you are and concentrate on moving. Treat it like any other rappel. Okay?"

I nod quickly and take in a deep breath. She's right – I have done this loads of times before, but that doesn't mean I have to like it. Feeling decidedly sick, I lean back, all the time saying a little prayer to whatever gods govern ropes and little bits of forged metal (it's times like this when agnosticism is preferable to atheism; there are just times in your life when, regardless of how sensible or cynical you are, sending up a little prayer is the only thing you can think of doing) and teeter over the edge. Fi flashes me another smile, but in the light of our headlamps, it looks more like a leer.

"You'll be fine."

Yeah. Sure.

I step off the edge.

My stomach swoops as my weight stabilises. There are no walls to guide me, so I tease the rope through the pulley, which in turn lowers me down in a series of small jerks, each one causing my heart to clunk against the inside of my ribcage. Above me, the small circle of Fi's headlamp grows smaller and smaller until there is nothing left but a pinprick, and I feel as if I am floating in space and her light is nothing more than a lonesome guiding star, cold and desolate.

Then something touches my boot and I scream. I can't help it.

"Hey... Hey... It's just us," Janos says as he and Marcus help me find my feet. I try to uncouple the clip, but my fingers won't work. In the end, Janos does it for me. He tugs on the now dangling rope and it begins its ascent, back up towards Fi.

"Are you all right?" Janos asks.

"Yeah," I say. "Yeah. Just... how deep are we?"

"About twenty feet."

"Twenty feet? Is that all?"

"Yes. But I know what you mean. It feels more. But rope lengths don't lie." He grins, and I find myself smiling back.

We wait a few minutes for Fi to rappel down. Brendan's already off, exploring the walls, despite Marcus telling him to fuckin' pack it in, we have to stay together, man, but he's lost in his own little world of wonder, and for a moment anyway, so am I.

The space we're in (it isn't a room; I can't think of it as a room, because if it's a room then someone lived here and that is the road where madness lies, my friend) is basically the same as the one above. Circular, with walls covered in weird pictograms. But there is one difference. Cut into the mineral is an archway.

And beyond that archway is a corridor.

We cluster around its entrance; our headlamps sweep the interior, making it resemble a particularly naff '90s rave. The walls are ribbed and soar up and over our heads, like a ribcage of some massive snake. The floor slopes downward a little, and the same apprehension from before grips me.

"It's the only way," Brendan says.

"I don't know..." I say. Every instinct is now screaming at me: don't go down there. I don't know why – hell, maybe I've developed a sudden and crushing case of claustrophobia – but it's all I can do from shinning straight back up that rope and taking my chances with the monster in the water. Which is saying a lot, because I have never once in my life successfully climbed a rope on my own without some kind of assistance.

"There is no other way," Janos says, cutting through my panicked train of thought. "And, come on – aren't you just a little curious?"

No. No, Janos, I am not. But I can see Brendan is, and even Fi is peering eagerly into the darkness ahead. Out of all of us, only Marcus shares my doubts, which is worrying. I mean, twice in one day? That's unheard of. But in the spirit of togetherness (and the fact that I have no desire to sit in the dark with Marcus), we all agree that we can't leave it – we have to at least have a look.

No one speaks as we creep down. The air feels flat down here, and there's a peculiar smell that sets my teeth on edge. I kind of recognise it… sort of. But there's not enough of it for me to identify it with any degree of certainty. That and I'm not sure there are many over-ripe bananas down there.

Even though it is pitch-dark, we all feel the shift in direction. We're no longer walking in a straight line, but rather the path is arcing, and it isn't long before I realise the path is forming a spiral, corkscrewing even deeper into the earth. We've been going for about half an hour or so when the darkness dissipates and a blue-tinged light filters up. With it come the smell, stronger now, and it no longer smelling of rotten bananas. Now it smells more of rancid meat. This causes all of us – even Brendan, whose growing hard-on for this place is getting quite disconcerting – to stop.

"Dead things?" Fi mouths.

We all shrug, because what else are you supposed to do?

With each step, the light grows in intensity until we can actually switch off our headlamps. This is a bit of a relief; even though we aren't reliant upon batteries due to our kinetic suits, there's always the unspoken risk of a bulb blowing, and thanks to Mr Monster in the Water, we don't have any spares. But even that relief is intermixed with doubt.

What's making the light?

We round the last corner and all stop as one.

In front of us is a room. Yes, this time I'm calling it a room. I can't keep kidding myself, because there is no doubt in my mind that this structure was once inhabited. By whom – or what – I don't know, but nature just doesn't make things like this.

It stretches out before us; a vast gallery bordered by… benches of some sort, and what I can only describe lamely as control panels. Above them, the walls have large sections cut out of them, and it is from them that the light comes. It is a rich oceanic turquoise, and it takes me a moment to figure out why... because they are windows, windows out into the ocean we have discovered, the ocean that swallowed Nik, the ocean that houses some kind of monster.

"Holy crap…" someone breathes behind me. I don't know who it is. I can't devote enough of my attention to figure it out. All I can do is stand and stare at what is laid out before me.

It looks like something from the set of some kind of sci-fi movie. The walls glisten with moisture, and moulded bumps adorn the panels beneath the windows. The 'benches' – I don't know what else to call them and have no idea what their true purpose might have been – are constructed out of the same material as the rest of the room, raised and moulded lumps that rise straight out of the floor. The whole thing reminds me of a laboratory, a feeling I can't shake off as we wander along the gallery, trying to fathom out what the strange nodules and spirals carved into the panels might mean.

"I knew it," Brendan says. "Alie-"

"Shut. Up," Marcus says. "Don't you dare say it. No one says it. This is fucked up enough without bringing that kind of… of bullshit into the equation."

I nod, unconsciously. Marcus is right. We have no idea what this place is, or what purpose it served. No one is to bandy the 'A' word around. No one.

"He has a point, though, Marcus," Fi says. "If it isn't, you know, them… then what? Who the hell built this? I mean, even if we've got the dating wrong and this place is… is… modern, what the hell is it? What does it do? And who the fuck owns it? I was in the military for ten years and worked on some pretty top-secret projects… but I haven't seen anything that even approaches this before. I don't even know where to start."

"Guys…" There's a guarded hint of worry to Janos's voice. I hadn't realised he had wandered off further into the room, I'm so mesmerised by what is all around me. He's crouching off just ahead of us in a darkened corner. And for the first time ever, he looks seriously worried.

"What is it?" I say.

"You'd better come over."

There it is again. That nasty knot in my guts that says 'no'. But I go over anyway. Janos stands up. He's switched his headlamp back on. I follow its beam. For the first time, I notice that the smell – that unpleasant rotted sweetness – is stronger in this corner.

At first, I can't quite work out what it is. It looks like a dark lump, full of curves and shadows. Then the curves begin to knit together, and the shadows define.

My hand flies to my mouth as I bite back the urge to gag.

It's a person.

And judging by the smell, they've been dead for a while.

Janos shakes his head, and his light strobes over the body.

"Who is it?" I whisper. It seems disrespectful to speak any louder.

"I don't know," Janos says. He steps back and allows the other three enough space to join us.

"Jesus," Fi says. Jesus, indeed. She hunkers down and tentatively pulls the body back. It flops back with an unpleasant squelch, and we all recoil as the stench intensifies.

"Ugh… how long do you think they've been here?" Marcus asks, his voice muffled by his arm.

Fi shakes her head. "It's hard to tell. There aren't any insects down here, and the – oh Jesus Christ, that smells horrible – atmospherics are unknown, so it could be, I dunno, a week? Give or take. I'm not an expert at this."

"Who is it?" I ask again.

"Looks like Clark," says Fi. "There's what looks like a tattoo on his wrist."

Janos nods.

"I think so too. Right height. Right… body shape." He swallows hard. "What are we going to do with him?"

"Nothing," Marcus says. "What can we do?"

He's got a point, but I can't help but feel it's wrong to leave him down here.

"Well, at least we know what happened to one of the Alpha Team," Brendan says.

"Do we?" I ask. "How did he die?"

Fi purses her lips and makes a weird smacking noise between her teeth; all the while, she is studying the body.

"Head trauma, I think," she indicates the back of his head. "There's a lot of blood there."

"So someone hit him over the head?" says Marcus.

"Either that or he… fell? Look, I don't know, and I wouldn't want to speculate. Either way, this doesn't fill me with confidence. Alpha Team were experts. That's why they were the Alpha Team. For this to happen to them is… disconcerting to say the least."

Fi pauses to chew on a hangnail, a sure sign that she is nervous. She quickly realises what she is doing and drops her hand. She knows that by displaying her nerves, she risks unsettling all of us. It isn't arrogance. It's a fact. Out of all of us, except maybe Janos, she is by far the most experienced, and is as tough as nails. I can't help but think that if she is disconcerted, the rest of us should be nothing short of downright terrified.

"So… where are the rest of them?" I ask. "We've found Clark… I can't see any other evidence of Alpha Team's presence at all."

"Maybe the thing in the water did get them," Brendan says, gazing out of the nearest window. It looks eerily calm out there. I have no idea what process is illuminating the water, but as I watch, I see small schools of fish dart past, little green-tinged lights twinkling down the sides of their bodies betraying their deep-sea heritage. One by one, we all turn to the window. We should be marvelling at what is laid out before us – who thought we'd find fish down here? – but we can't. Everything is too huge, too surreal, to allow us even to contemplate what we are experiencing.

Other small things dart past, little squid-like things about eight inches long. They have huge eyes and are a mottled grey in colour. Janos steps towards the pane, his brows drawn.

"Belemnites? He says. He voices it like a question, even though we know he doesn't mean it. "There's a whole Jurassic ecosystem out there."

As if on command, something large and fast darts out of the blue. It's about eight feet long, with a streamlined, dolphin-like body. It snaps up a mouthful of the belemnite creatures and then with a flick of its tail, it's gone.

I can't breathe properly. I know what that was. I've seen fossil ones nearly everywhere. The Posidonienschiefer is full of them.

"Ichthyosaur," I whisper. Janos faces me and nods, his expression curiously slack.

“This place is amazing,” Brendan says. “It’s like the ocean time forgot. We're so lucky!”

The rest of us glance back to the sad remains of Raymond Clark, caving expert, extreme survivalist. He wasn't so lucky. Once upon a time, I would have agreed with Brendan. Now, all I want to do is get away and forget it ever existed.

Chapter Six

We watch for a few minutes longer, but nothing else makes an appearance. Well, why should they? It's a big stretch of water out there. By silent agreement, we decide to leave Clark's remains where they are. What would be the point in moving them? It's not like we could take them back to his loved ones. We haven't even worked out how to reach our radio, let alone a strategy that might get us out of this place.

At the other end of the galley is another ribbed corridor. This one is shorter, and after only one turn of the corkscrew, there's another archway with more blue light spilling from it.

This room isn't as large as the gallery upstairs (heh, funny how you think of those things in such human terms even when blatantly not human. We haven't come across anything resembling a bathroom, and there aren't even any stairs) but it is no less impressive. This one is square with a circular design carved into the floor. Around it, sit six huge chair-like constructions, like thrones for kings of old.

And in one, sits a figure.

The suffocating feeling is back. The quality of the light isn't so great that we can make out any details, but it's obvious whoever (or whatever) it is, they're too small for what they're sitting on.

"H… hello?" Janos calls out. His usually steady voice cracks a little. "Who is it?"

There is no reply.

He takes a tentative step into the room. Nothing stirs.

"Hello?" he tries again.

Nothing.

Fi follows him, then me, then Brendan, and finally Marcus, who has his arms wrapped around himself as if he's trying to seek comfort from them.

Still the figure does not move.

"Is it… dead?" I ask.

Janos doesn't answer. Instead, he continues to creep forward.

"Oh, dear sweet Lord… Yuri?"

Yuri? What? Then it dawns on me. Yuri Blavatsky. Another member of the Alpha Team. Now I can't breathe fast enough. My heart drives my lungs like a piston until I feel as if I am going to pass out.

"Oh, no," Fi whispers, and picks up the pace to draw level with Janos. "Is he…"

"What do you think? Does he look alive to you?" Despite the panic that grips me, I can't help but feel for Janos. Yuri was his friend. They'd climbed together a lot in the past, and mapped out a huge virgin cave system in Bolivia together.

"He doesn't smell," Brendan says, and I almost slap him for his insensitivity. What a thing to say.

Again, we gather around the corpse of an Alpha Team member. A curious feeling of deja-vu settles over me. Yuri is sitting with his eyes closed, his teeth gritted. In death, he had gripped the arms of the chair, and it looks like he never let go. It's weird. He kind of looks like one of those pictures of astronauts during their high velocity training, testing to see how many Gs they can withstand. Fi shakes her head, and Marcus wipes his mouth with one hand to disguise the way his jaw is trembling. Even Brendan has the courtesy to glance down at the floor in respect. Janos mutters something under his breath – a prayer, I guess – and leans over to touch Yuri on the arm.

At this slight pressure, Yuri's body begins to convulse. We all jump back, uttering barks of shock. My heart just about gives up when Yuri starts to scream, his eyes now wide open and staring.

"Oh, dear Jesus – he's alive!" Marcus whispers, both his hands covering his face, like a small child hiding from the Bogeyman.

"Help him!" Janos pleads. "Help him!"

I don't know what to do. The desire is there, but I'm rooted to the spot, paralysed. Yuri is trying to wrench his hands from the chair, but they're stuck fast. Fi muscles in and grabs one of his arms whilst Yuri keeps emitting high-pitched shrieks. She pulls, but nothing happens. Janos takes his other arm and mimics Fi, but it's no use. Yuri's whole body continues to shake and blood streams from his left nostril. Marcus and I share a helpless, terrified look.

Then, as quickly as it began, it's over. Something in the chair clicks, and Yuri's hands are released. Fi topples over – she was still trying to free him. Yuri slumps forward.

"Is he…" Brendan asks.

Janos reaches out with a shaking hand and presses two fingers against the side of Yuri's neck. He shakes his head.

"No. He's alive. Just."

Fi and Janos help Yuri out of the chair. He's out cold. He looks gaunt, lying their stretched out on the floor, and the blood from his nostril is smeared all over the lower half of his face, making him look like some cheap make-up job in a zombie B movie. It's clear from the way we all stare at him that none of us has a clue what to do. Yeah, we all took the advanced first aid course, but (unsurprisingly) that doesn't cover finding emaciated team mates trapped in a murder chair.

"We can't leave him here," Janos says after a long stretch of silence. I find myself nodding in unconscious agreement.

"We may not have a choice," Fi says. Janos snaps his head around angrily, but before he can protest, Fi continues. "He's barely alive. He's definitely too weak to even contemplate trying to get him back to the other shore."

"But we can't leave him here," Janos says, again. "He needs proper medical attention-"

"You think I can't see that? Hey, anyone got a cell phone? Maybe I should just dial up 911 and get an ambulance down here." Fi's tone drips with sarcasm and I wince when Janos's expression hardens.

"If we leave him here, he will die," Janos says through gritted teeth.

"And if we take him out there, he'll die. Either way, we're potentially looking at another corpse. In the long run, this is the best place for him."

In the long run? No. But for the time being, I have to agree with Fi. I can understand Janos's desire to get his friend out of this place, but whether he likes it or not, this is the safest place for him.

"Look, Janos... I get it, okay? I get it." Fi risks reaching out and touching him on the arm. He tenses for a moment and we all hold our breath, but instead of punching her, Janos lets out a long, defeated sigh. "Until one of us can get to the radio and let Rescue know what has happened here, I say we don't move him. We keep him as comfortable as we can and…" she trails off.

No one says anything to that. No one has to. We take it in turns to explore the rest of the room. We decided pretty quickly that one of us should stay with Yuri whilst everyone else went off, but it was clear from the way everyone glanced at him that no one really wanted to be the one told they have to stay. So, in the end, we sort out a little system, a tried and tested method to settle difficult decisions the world over. We drew straws.

I picked the short one.

"We'll be back soon," Janos says, and pats me on the shoulder. "Promise."

Fi gives me a wry smile and the four of them set off, exploring the room and the environs beyond. All the while I can hear them, I'm kind of okay. Yuri's breathing is shallow but steady, and there's enough light in here for me to get my notebook out. Huh. Isn't that ironic? We've lost every other way of communication apart from the written word. I must remember to write to Steadmarsh & Sons and commend them on their field journals – they really are waterproof and capable of withstanding any environment.

Without anything else to do, I sit cross-legged on the cold floor and begin to jot down my thoughts, which are nothing more than random words. Lost. Ancient? Who built this? Technology beyond anything humanity is capable of. I think. Does anything still work? Who? Why? What is in the water? Is it natural?

Are we doing to die down here?

I stare at the last question. Well, are we? I don't know if I'm ready to even contemplate the answer. At the moment, everything feels so surreal; I'm still waiting to wake up. Well, maybe that's it. Maybe this is just a really vivid anxiety dream, and in reality, I'm still back at the barracks, fast aslee-

"Water…"

I drop my pencil.

"…water…"

"Oh my God. Oh, dear Lord. Yuri? Are you okay?" My notebook tumbles from my hands as I scrabble forwards. Yuri's eyes are still closed, but his lips are moving.

"…water…"

Water. Of course. He's been stuck in that chair. I fight with the strap of my water canister and shakily hold it out. Oh, right, yeah. Way to go, Meg. Exactly how is he going to hold it? I'm going to have to hold his head up and feed it to him. But the thought of touching him makes my skin crawl. I feel ashamed to say that, but it's the truth.

"Guys?" I call out. "Guys? Where are you? It's Yuri. He's awake." I try (and fail) to keep the panic out of my voice. "Guys?!"

"…water…"

"Hang on, Yuri, just hang in there…"

Oh, get a grip, girl! The man needs water, and you're dithering because he looks like he's sick? This could be it – if you don't help him now, he could die. Then what would the others think? But the thought of touching his bony neck, of cradling his blood covered head with its papery, grey skin, makes me feel ill.

"…please…"

His eyes flutter open, exposing yellowing corneas. He's trying to look at me, at the person who is at once his saviour and his torturer. I reach out to him, but snatch my hand back just before I can touch him.

"Come on, Meg," I tell myself. "He's another person. He needs your help. Come on, you can do this..."

This time, I slide my hand under his neck. The skin there feels surprisingly smooth. Despite his ragged appearance, Yuri isn't an old man, so I don't know why I'm surprised. I swallow down a bloom of bile, disgusted with myself that I've even reacted in that way. He lets out a long, hissing sigh and I almost drop him in shock.

"Oh, dear Jesus... no. No. Get it together, Meg. Keep going."

I keep talking to myself, my internal cheerleader back flipping and pom-pom shaking for all she is worth. Finally, I raise my water bottle to Yuri's dry lips and trickle a small amount over them. Most of it runs down his chin, but some hits the mark. I feel him swallow.

"…more…"

I tip the bottle a little more. His gulps are stronger now. I begin to calm down a little, feeling better that I did the right thing. A little part of me frets that I might do him some damage by giving him too much water, but sod it. Too much water is infinitely better than not enough.

Yuri's looking at me now through heavy eyes. My brief moment of do-gooder self-satisfaction is punctured. I don't like the way he is looking at me. Like I'm not really there-

His hand shoots up and grabs me by the back of my neck. It happens so fast, I can't even squawk out a protest. I drop the canister, and water spills down his front, but he doesn't seem to care. He drags my face close to his, and I can feel the heat of his breath upon my cheek.

"So cold…" he whispers. "So long. In there. I know. I saw. They did it. They're here. In here. Cold now."

Finally, I find my voice and let out a ragged screech. It feels like my heart is in my head, pounding against my temples as Yuri keeps on babbling, sometimes in English, sometimes in Russian, a jumbled mash I can't follow.

"Meg!" A voice calls out, a blessed, beautiful voice that isn't mine or this mad man's. Another pair of hands grasps me and prises Yuri's skeletal fingers from the back of my neck, allowing me to scramble backwards. Yuri lets out a bark of laughter and slumps back to the ground whilst I battle down a huge, salty lump in my throat. I'm not going to cry. That just isn't an option. Not going to cry. Not going to.

"Are you all right?" Janos asks.

Okay, so maybe I am going to cry. I don't want to, but I can't help it. Janos wraps an arm around my shoulders and pulls my head to his chest. Part of me wants to pull back, but another, bigger part of me knows this is exactly what I need.

I hear running footsteps approach.

"What the hell happened?" Marcus asks.

"I heard Megan scream," Janos says. "So I ran back. Yuri... Yuri..."

From his prone position on the floor, Yuri giggles.

"He's awake?"

"Oh yeah," I say. "He's awake. He... He attacked me."

"What?" Marcus sounds shocked.

"I don't think it was an attack," Janos says. I pull away from him, a sudden flush of fury filling me.

"Oh, and I suppose you saw enough to come to that conclusion, did you? You were close enough to see what was in his eyes?"

"Megan, calm down," Janos says. "He grabbed you, yes – but did he hurt you? Really?"

I rub the back of my neck. No, I suppose not. He might have scared the hell out of me, but he didn't hurt me. Not really. But, for some reason, I don't really want to admit that to Janos. So, instead, I shrug. Good old shrug. Answers everything.

***

I don't know if it was the shock of discovering Yuri, or simply that we'd been on the go for over 12 hours, but after that, it was decided unanimously that we needed to rest. Another unanimous decision was that we'd rest outside the tower. Luckily, the ropes were fine (I spent at least half of the 45 minute trudge back up to the hole fretting that they'd been damaged in some way, or worse, had disappeared), and our only major obstacle was Yuri, who in the end had to be tied into the ropes and hauled up manually.

Still, we're up here now. Not that 'up here' is any better. The tower still looms over us. No one is going to rest with that thing nearby. So, despite our exhaustion, we trek back to the shoreline, back to where there is at least a little bit of light.

Nothing burns, so we're sitting in the almost dark, huddled against one of the outcrops that borders the little cove we arrived in. It's frustrating. The distance between here and the opposite beach is nothing. Nothing. I swim that in the pool everyday, and then some. I could get over there in what, ten minutes? No, less. Five. Then I hear the faint splashing of something breaking the water's surface, and I'm brought back down to earth. It isn't the distance that's the problem. It's what's in it.

Whatever it is.

We're still debating. Janos is pretty much stuck on the pliosaur hypothesis, and based on the tooth we had (thanks, Marcus), I am reluctantly with him. Fi is undecided. She says she can't deny something big and predatory is out there, but won't commit to any firm theory. Brendan is convinced it is something totally new to science (which in his defence, it might be, you never know. Stranger things have happened. I mean, look at us right now), but the way he talks about it makes me feel a bit uncomfortable. He's a bit too keen. Marcus, on the other hand, is Brendan's opposite. He's adamant we're all nuts and there's nothing out there, but when we offer the chance to swim the short distance to the other shore, he's quick to shake his head and refuse, so we know he's talking crap and he knows it.

Then there's Yuri. We've tried asking him where the rest of his team are, but it's no use. Every time anyone mentions them, his eyes go glassy. The rest of the time, he listens to us intently, his head cocked like a demented pigeon. At first, he doesn't say anything, but when Brendan the Believer gets into a bit of a verbal sparring match with Marcus the Sceptic, he starts to giggle, this weird, snorty sound that he tries to muffle with his hands. It makes my skin crawl.

"What is it, Yuri?" Janos asks gently. Out of all of us, he's the only one who doesn't seem totally freaked out by Yuri's complete mental collapse.

Again, Yuri says nothing, just keeps giggling.

"What the fucking hell is wrong with him?" Marcus asks. He's already on edge, and the last thing he – and we – need is this additional madness. "Okay, so he was trapped down here, but it was only for what, a week? Ten days? No one goes this nuts that quickly."

"So, what? You think he's faking it?" Fi asks.

He steals a glance at Yuri, who is back to staring into space. He shudders.

"No… no, I'm not saying that. What I am saying is something else must have happened to him."

"Like being attached by an alien species from the deep?" Brendan says.

"Fuck off," Marcus snaps. "That's enough of your bull. No. Something else."

"Besides, that happened to us, and we're, uh, okay." I say, and then wonder exactly how true that claim is when I see the look Marcus gives Brendan.

Fi must've seen it too, because her brows crease and she shoots me a worried glance. She doesn't have to say anything else. We're going to have to keep an eye on those two.

"No, Marcus is right," Janos says. "Something else has happened here." He gets up and crouches in front of Yuri, and mutters something I don't understand in Russian. The effect on Yuri is electric. He sits bolt upright and whispers something back. Tears spring in his eyes, and then he claps his hand over his month. Janos frowns.

"Well, what did he say?" Marcus asks. Janos holds one hand up, the universal plea for patience. He says something else in Russian – it sounds like a question, but I can't be too sure. Yuri shakes his head violently and giggles again, his eyes still bright with tears. He whispers something again, but as he goes on, he gets louder and louder until he jumps up and starts yelling. Janos springs to his feet and grasps Yuri by his shoulders, obviously trying to calm him down, but now he is screaming, punching the air in the direction of the water, spittle flying from his lips.

Then, as quickly as the outburst began, it ends. Yuri crumples to the floor, rolls himself up into a foetal position and refuses to move.

***

No one really knew what to say after that. Every now and again, a whimper would escape Yuri and we'd all jump, just a little bit. Marcus went to ask something, but Fi silenced him with one of her laser stares. Problem was, that meant we had nothing to talk about, and the silence was doing my head in, so in the end, I sparked up a totally inane conversation about what we were missing on TV that night, which didn't really work considering we're from all over the place so didn't have a clue what each other was on about half the time, but it did allow us to focus on something that wasn't either depressing, terrifying or an interesting mix of both.

One by one, exhaustion overtook us. Brendan was the first to succumb, followed by Marcus, who snored like a bastard until Fi kicked him. Yuri was still curled up in a tight ball, and we left him there. I mean, what else were we supposed to do? Finally, I gave in to the hot, scratchy feeling in my eyes and lay back, hovering in that weird, floaty place between sleep and wakefulness. I sensed someone sit down next to me, and it took a real effort to crack one eye open.

Janos.

"Are you all right?" he asks, his voice barely above a whisper.

I nod. As badly as things are going, I suppose I'm coping pretty well. I mean, I managed to sleep. Kind of.

Janos nods back. Now, I may not be the best at reading people, but even I can see something is bugging him.

"You all right?" I ask.

He pauses. His jaw works, and he frowns a bit, obviously trying to figure out what to say next.

"I don't know," he says eventually. "Yuri… he is worrying me."

You and me, brother. In our exhaustion, none of us really bothered to find out what Yuri had said. Most of that is because we knew whatever it was, it would be madness, but a small fragment is also because we fear he might actually talk perfect sense.

"Yeah. Me too. Marcus is right. He shouldn't have gone quite that nuts in such a short space of time."

"Especially since he was a member of the Spetsnaz," Janos says. "He is used to operating under pressure. That is one of the reasons he was chosen over me for the Alpha team."

"He was chosen over you?"

Janos nods.

"I didn't know that."

"Why would you? It's not important."

"Do you… do you know him well? I know you were both part of the team that went to Bolivia and everything."

Janos pauses again. "Well enough to consider him a friend. And well enough to know that this… episode is not normal. He is the sanest of the sane."

"Uh, not now, he isn't," I say.

"No, not now, but once he was." Janos breaks off again and stares in Yuri's direction. The Russian still hasn't moved, and for a moment, I wonder if he is dead. Then I catch the almost imperceptible movement of his back, indicating that he is indeed still alive.

"He says… he says…" Janos stops, struggling.

"He says what?" I prompt.

"He says… in that chair… it wasn't just a chair. He says he was shown things."

"Shown things? Like what?"

"Time." A soft voice croaks in the darkness. Both Janos and I look back over to Yuri. He's rolled over and is staring back at us. "I was shown time."

I frown and glance to Janos, who gives me a tiny shake of his head.

"What do you mean, Yuri?" I ask.

Yuri gets to his hands and knees and crawls towards us. I suppress the urge to skitter away from him. I know what has happened to him isn't his fault, but I can't help it. He creeps me out.

He stops next to us and throws a haunted look at the rest of our slumbering party, likes he's worried he will be overheard.

"They did it. They built this place. A long time ago. A long, long, long time ago. They came here. Wasn't suitable. Life not… advanced enough. They tried. Tried to accelerate it. But it didn't work. So they left. Went back. Back to the spaces in between."

"They… left?" I don't have a clue what he was blithering on about, and I'm not sure I really want to know. It sounds like a mixture of Brendan's mad alien conspiracy theories and something you might watch on one of the less reputable cable TV channels. "Who are they?"

Yuri snorts and covers his mouth with his hands, as if trying to cram whatever was trying to get out back in. He mutters something in Russian. Janos leans forward, and Yuri whispers to him furiously.

"He says…" Janos closes his eyes for a moment and swallows. "He says they are here."

Yuri nods, his eyes wide and staring. "Here."

"That's not what I asked," I say. "And what does he mean, 'here'? I thought he said they went?"

"Yes, yes," Yuri says. "They went. Away. Back. No time there. Can see everything. Everywhere. Every when. I saw. They showed me. Everything."

Yuri leaps to his feet, making me jump.

"I saw it all! The beginning, the end, what lies outside and in!" He is no longer whispering now, but shouting. Everyone else wakes with a start, complaining loudly as Yuri scampers around, babbling in a mixture of Russian and English about stars and atoms and them, those who know, who live, who die; yet do not live at all. Fi jumps up looking furious and grabs him, but he throws her off as if she is nothing more than an annoying five year old playing 'bundle'. In the end, it takes both Janos and Fi to subdue him whilst Marcus swears and Brendan and I stare in horror at just how damaged Yuri is.

As quickly as it began, it ends. It's as if Yuri just gives up. He lies on the ground and mutters something that turns my blood to ice: "That is not dead which can eternal lie…"

He closes his eyes, and nothing we do can rouse him.

Janos and Fi hold on to him for a moment longer, just in case, but it's clear he has entered whatever catatonic state he was in before.

"We have to get him out of here," Fi says, running her hands over her shorn head. "We can't watch him 24/7, nor can we give him what he needs."

"He needs to be shot," Marcus says. "Fucking nut case. What was all that he was yelling about?"

"He does not need to be shot," Janos says, angry. "He is sick. He needs treatment. He's been through something none of us have a hope of understanding."

"We don't have a hope? I should coco! You want to understand that? Count me out," Marcus says.

"That's rich, coming from you," Janos says. "You whined like a child when you were passed over for Alpha team. 'Oh it is not fair, oh I have all the experience, I'm fit, I'm seasoned, oh I-"

"Shut up!" Marcus takes a step toward Janos, squaring up to him. "Yeah, I wanted to be part of Alpha team, but I seem to remember you being just as pissed off as me at being passed over, so just shut the fuck up-"

"Guys," Fi says, holding up her hands in an attempt at placating them. "Come on"

"No, Fi – no. I've got a wife. I've got kids. I am not even going to entertain the crap you lot are spouting. I just want out. I just want to leave. I don't care if you think I'm a coward, I just want to see my family again."

His eyes glisten in the meagre half-light, and I suddenly feel very sorry for Marcus indeed. He might be a blustering idiot sometimes, but he's right. He does have a wife and kids who love him, and the thought of them stuck back home, waiting for news, any news, as to what might have happened to him makes my throat feel tight.

"Look, Marcus, no one thinks you're a coward." I begin, but Marcus throws a hand up in my direction.

"No, don't even say it. I don't want to hear it. I don't want to hear any of it. I just want to leave."

"Okay. Fine. Well, off you go then." Obviously, Fi isn't feeling the same sympathy for him that I am. "If all of this is crap and you don't want to hear anything from any of us – it's a short distance. Go on. Swim across. Get the radio." She sticks her jaw out belligerently.

Marcus's eyes dart from Fi to me, then to Janos and finally to Brendan, looking for some kind of support. I want to tell him it's okay, but I find the weight of the moment stills my tongue. His eyes harden.

"Okay. All right. It's all bullshit. I'm going." He stalks towards the water's edge and rolls his shoulders, as if preparing to dive in. My heart leaps to my throat as he takes a tentative step forwards into the frigid water. It might be my imagination, but I think I hear the slop of disturbed water up ahead, as if something large had surfaced and then sunk back into the depths. If Marcus heard anything, he's not letting on. Instead, he wades knee high into the water.

That's enough to break my paralysis. I don't care what he thinks, I'm not going to watch one of us sacrifice ourselves simply to protect a bruised ego.

"Marcus," I say, and walk towards the shore. "Stop it. Just leave it. No one thinks you're a coward. We're all in this ridiculous situation, and we're all stressed and frightened. So… please. Please. Come out of the water."

He pauses. I can feel everyone behind me hold their breath, even Fi. I know she had no intention of baiting him into doing this. As I said, it's stress. It makes us all do strange things.

At first, I think Marcus is going to ignore me, but then it happens again. That weird slapping sound, on the edge of our hearing. This time, it's followed by a snort, as if a large animal was taking in a breath.

Even from here, I see Marcus's Adams apple bob as he swallows. He backs off, towards me, into shallower water. Another slap in the distance sends him skittering the last few feet out of the water and back on to dry land.

"What is it?" he says, very quietly, to me. He seems deflated now, as if all his previous bile and spite has been knocked out of him. I know I said he was a pain in the arse before, but I think I preferred that version of Marcus to this new, subdued one.

"I don't know," I say, because that is the truth. I don't know. "Come on."

"I just want to see my family again," he says.

"I know. I know. We all do. See our own families, that is. It would be a bit weird if we all wanted to see your family."

Marcus snorts at this, and wipes his nose with the back of his hand.

"Yeah, that would be odd." He pauses. "Thanks, Meg."

"It's okay. Let's just go and get some rest. Maybe things will look better after we've had some sleep."

***

But things didn't look better after we'd had some sleep. With no sun to guide us, our body clocks are screwed, and so we all felt as tired upon waking up as we did before we went to sleep.

Food is also becoming an issue, and the less said about the water situation, the better. In the end, Brendan and Fi go off and recover some very dodgy looking shellfish from the rocks that border the lake, which we jimmy open with knives and eat raw. I try to pretend mine is good sashimi.

It doesn't work.

"I've been thinking," Fi says, through a mouthful of squishy mollusc. "I think it's safe to say that, despite our personal reservations, we can all agree that there is something in that lake. Something big. But it isn't something that can be everywhere at once. One way or another, we're going to have to find a way off this rock." She stops short of adding the qualifier 'before we either die of thirst or starvation', and I'm grateful for that. No point emphasising the obvious.

"So, what are you saying?" Brendan asks.

"I'm saying we need to distract it. The distance between here and the shore isn't that far. I could swim across that in minutes. I already would have if I knew exactly what it was we're up against."

"Okay, genius – that's great, but how do we distract it?" Marcus says.

It might just be my imagination, but I think I catch a glimpse of smugness flit across Fi's face.

"I've been thinking about my training. Whilst I haven't had much experience in dealing with monsters from the black lagoon," she pauses, waiting for one of us to at least chuckle. We don't. Unfazed, she continues on, "Uh yeah, anyway, I have had some training for diving with sharks. Now I know the chances of this thing being some kind of shark are pretty slim, but I wonder if we could employ the same tactics."

"Tactics?" I ask.

"Yeah. Everyone knows that you can use movement to attract sharks. You know, vibrations in the water. I'm guessing that thing uses similar tactics."

No one disagrees with her. After all, hadn't that thing attacked the boat? How else would it have known we were there? It couldn't have known to associate the smell of rubber with prey, and it's pitch black down here so eyesight is pretty much useless – so what's the next thing on the list? Acoustics. Vibrations. It makes sense.

"That's fine and dandy, but short of us all swimming across together and hoping one of us survives 'cos this thing's going after the other, I don't get your point," says Marcus.

"That's where I've been thinking a little ahead of you," says Fi, again with the smug look. Marcus bristles, and Janos and I exchange a concerned look. Like we really need this again.

"Oh, really?"

"Yeah, really."

"Fi? Marcus? Can we please leave the posturing at the door and just get to the point?" says Janos. His voice sounds heavy and tired. I know exactly how he feels.

For a moment, it looks like Marcus is going to bite back, but instead, he sighs and sits back.

"Okay, this is my idea," Fi says with all together too much enthusiasm. "We all have rope, yeah? And there are plenty of loose rocks and shit around. I say we go over to the headland with a bunch of those heavy rocks tied to the ends of the rope. We can also take more to chuck in, to make one hell of a disturbance."

"So, what you're saying is… chuck rocks into the water?" Marcus asks.

"Well… basically, yes –"

Even I could quite happily slap her for that one. What an idiotic idea. Chuck rocks in the water. Like that's going to make a difference.

"Look, I know you all think I've lost it," Fi says, "but what other choice do we have? We can sit here and kid ourselves that any movement we think we may or may not have seen is down to currents or whatever, but is anyone willing to wade in and test that hypothesis? Even if they were, I'd stop them, because we all know there's something in the water. We need something else. A distraction."

"By chucking rocks in the water?" I say. I know they say desperate times call for desperate measures, but this has gone too far. "Even if its hunting strategy is based on vibration, it'll also be using smell. They don't just chuck stuff in the sea to catch sharks – they chum it, too…"

I trail off. The look Fi is giving me now is making me feel ever so slightly uncomfortable. It's sort of caught directly between shame and triumph, which is a weird place to be.

"Yeah, of course. But I've thought of that, too," she says. "Obviously, even if the creature is attracted by the racket we're making, there's still a good chance it might smell whoever is swimming and go for them anyway. So we need, uh, chum, too."

"Chum?" Marcus says, flatly. "And exactly where are we going to get hold of that? We're not exactly swamped with fishing gear, and whilst there's quite a lot of shellfish out there, I'm not sure… whatever it is will choose mussels over a nice juicy human."

There it is again. That look of shame and triumph. She's already thought of that, obviously.

Then it hits me.

"Oh, no. No. You can't be serious?" I say. "That's… inhuman. Sacrilegious. No way."

"I know it's distasteful, Meg – but do you have a better plan? It's not as if he's going anywhere-"

"What?" says Janos. By the look on his face, he's twigged on to Fi's plan, too. "That's monstrous!"

"Monstrous or not, it's the only plan we have," Fi says.

"Hey, hey, hang on – what plan?" Marcus asks.

"Haven't you worked it out, yet?" I say. "We need 'chum'. Which in the real world are half-rotten bits of fish. Now we don't have any half-rotten fish lying about, but we do have…"

A little light dawns in Marcus's eyes, followed by a disgusted grimace.

"You mean… Clark? Use Clark as chum? Oh, man – that's sick!"

"As sick as it might be – what other choice do we have? Clark is dead. He doesn't need his body, which is currently bloating up quite nicely down there. Whatever stink that creates, it'll be a far more attractive prospect than whoever is swimming across the strait-“

“You hope,” I mutter.

Fi glares at me.

“And so who is going to do this noble deed, then?” Marcus asks, his voice dripping with sarcasm. This is one time when I’m actually happy he has such a hard time hiding his emotions. “You know, hacking up a dead man and dropping him into the water to either lie in pieces on the seabed, or be snapped up by some ancient monster of the deep? Because I’ll tell you one thing – it ain’t gonna be me!”

“Well, if you’re going to be squeamish-“

“It isn’t about being fucking squeamish,” Marcus says. “It’s about respect for the dead! Jesus, Fiona, you are a real piece of work sometimes.”

“And exactly what do you mean by that?” Fi asks.

“You know exactly what I mean. Sometimes I wonder if you need to get yourself checked out. You know, make sure everything is where it should be-“

“Fuck off, Marcus,” Fi snaps. They glare at each other and I can’t help but feel there’s more to this exchange than I realised. I always thought Fi and Marcus got on – when Nik was with us, I always got the impression they resented me, Brendan and Janos’s intrusion into their cosy little set up. Oh well, only goes to show, you know what thought did…

“He does make a good point, though,” Janos breaks in. “Who is going to do it? I suggest Fi, since it is her idea.”

At first, Fi doesn’t say anything, and I wonder if she’s going to try to wriggle out of it. In a way, she does.

“I’ll help bring Clark’s body up,” she says, “But since I’ll be the one swimming, I can’t get involved with the, er, chumming.”

“So, you’ll swim?” Marcus says. He doesn’t sound angry now. If anything, he sounds worried. First three, then two, down to one and that jazz. I can see it going through his mind.

“I’m the best swimmer here,” she says, without a trace of pride because we all know it’s true. Her Marine training means, when it comes to the physical stuff, Fi’s pretty formidable. “I'd skip across that strait in what… five minutes? Seven, tops? With you lot feeding the beast over the other side of the headland, I'll just go hell for leather. Get over there. Should be a piece of cake."

Yeah. A piece of cake. And if it wasn't for the tremble in her voice, I might have believed her. But as it was, I didn't. I don't. She's clutching at straws, and she knows it. Anything to get out of here.

"Look… Look… why don't we just sit on this for a while?" I say. "We've been here, what, a day? Thirty-six hours max? It's not that long. Okay, sure, it's not exactly the Ritz, and the supply issue is an, uh, issue, but if we leave it a little longer, then maybe the thing'll just go away. Why else would it hang around here?" I gesture to the vast stretch of open water beyond the headland. "He's got all of that to hunt in. All of that versus this tiny strait. I'm guessing if it is as big as we think it is, it's going to need big prey. Much bigger than a human. We're over-estimating its intelligence. Give it another day and it'll move off. It'll get hungry and go and look for more suitable prey."

"And how do we know that it's gone?" Fi asks. "You think I haven't thought of this? Meg, we could be here all fucking year, and might never work out exactly what that thing is or what its habits are. Another train of thought is that the strait is deep, making it a perfect ambush spot. What if we're sitting right on top of its lair? What if it doesn't leave because this is home sweet home? Then all we've done is deplete our already dwindling supplies by sitting on our hands. No. I say we do this. We do this now..." *...Before I lose my nerve.*

She didn't have to say it, but I know that's what she meant. And judging by the slow, serious nods Janos and Marcus are giving her, they know it, too.

"Hey – where's Yuri?"

Brendan hasn't spoken in so long, I kind of forgot he was with us. We all turn and he's right – Yuri is nowhere to be seen.

"Oh, shit," Fi says. "Where the fuck has he gone?"

"We have to find him," Janos says. "Who knows what he will do?

"Throw himself off the cliff, if we have any luck," Marcus mutters.

No one has the energy to rebuke him. Instead, we split up – I know every single trope out there says not to, but the danger was in the water, not on the island… well, at least we hope it isn't on the island – and worked our way out, calling his name. In the end, Brendan found him, gazing over the water from the island's highest spot, grinning like an idiot.

I don't know what he told Brendan, but by the time we all arrived, Brendan was gazing with him, as if trying to spot something. When we asked him what he was looking at, he just shook himself and smiled, telling us it was nothing, just humouring Yuri until we all arrived to take care of him, but I'm not so sure. There's a wistfulness to Brendan's gaze that unnerves me. I don't think this is a very healthy place for Brendan. I mean, it's not exactly a health spa for the rest of us… but, I don't know. Something tells me Brendan's the one to watch.

With Yuri back with us, the others soon fall to arguing who is going to recover Clark's body. If I'm honest, I'm only too happy to stand on the side lines and watch. I don't care what Fi says, or how much Janos tries to rationalise it – I don't like this. And judging by the grim look on Marcus's face, neither does he. In the end, it is decided that Janos, Marcus and Fi will retrieve the body, using the remains of the dinghy to wrap it in.

Brendan and I will watch Yuri.

Actually, on second thought, I think I'd like to be on body duty.

***

As it happens, Yuri didn't give us much trouble. We kept him away from the structure as going anywhere near to that white tower causes him to lapse into mutters, punctuated with the occasion shriek, and instead, we managed to keep him calm by letting him watch the water.

Brendan, though… he's a different matter. He's definitely worrying me. He keeps looking back to the tower, as if it's going to suddenly do something quite spectacular. When I question him – gently – about what he's thinking, he jumps as if bitten and gives me a half-arsed response about how he's just interested, considering everything. Interested. Yeah. Because standing there, muttering to yourself whilst giving a weird building what can only be described as 'loving looks' is totally the definition of 'interested'.

It takes the others nearly an hour to get Clark's body to the ropes. I kind of feel like a stressed out mother trying to keep an eye on two toddlers as I flit between Yuri and Brendan. I'm not sure I can trust either of them.

Brendan informs me the others are ready and that they're calling from the antechamber. By the sound of it, they're getting quite insistent.

"Meg? Brendan? Where are you?"

It's Fi.

"For fuck's sake!"

Yep, Marcus.

"Hey… sorry," I say, and peer into the darkness. "Why haven't you all just climbed up?"

"Not that simple," says Fi. She emerges from the darkness looking stressed, and even though I knew she was there, my heart still jolts at her sudden appearance. "We've tied Clark's body as best we can to the harnesses, but it's going to be an… interesting job. Where are the other two?"

Now this is a good question.

"Yuri's watching the water again. And Brendan… I dunno. I think all of this is getting a bit much for him."

"And you think it isn't for the rest of us?"

"No… no… that's not what I mean. Surely, you've noticed it? I mean, I know he has far more caving experience than I do, but even I can see that something's not right with him. He keeps staring at this place and talking to himself."

I hear a sigh followed by a mutter from below.

"Yeah, we've noticed," Fi says. She wanders to the door and looks out. There's not much to see – she certainly won't be able to spy Yuri, and I doubt Brendan's visible, either, but she still looks. For a split second, she looks older than her years, and tired. "I'll be honest, I thought if anyone was going to lose it, it would be, well, you know…"

"Me?" I say.

"Yeah. Sorry, but you're the one with the least caving experience. But Brendan… okay, so he's a pup, there's no getting away from that, but cave ecology is his thing. He shouldn't be going loopy, not yet, anyway."

"I wouldn't say he's gone loopy, as such…" I begin. Fi interrupts me with a chuckle.

"Okay, so, no, not loopy. But definitely 'conspiracy theory', anyway. It's the reason I think the sooner we get out of here the better, and if that means taking a risk…"

She trails off. Even I can see she's scared. I don't blame her. A risk? Borderline suicidal, more like. This is it. All or nothing. If she succeeds, then we're fine. If she doesn't… yeah. I don't think I need to draw a picture.

Together, Fi and I carefully haul up the ropes. Tied at the base is a jumble of ragged rubber and a whiff of something that makes my stomach heave. It takes everything I've got to untie Clark's body, and even more to lift it out of the way. The body is heavy, but it has more to do with my unwillingness to touch him, even if he is wrapped up. Everything about this feels wrong, but we're nearly there. Plus, I don't think Fi would cope if I chickened out now.

We send the ropes back down, which Marcus and Janos scramble back up. A few minutes later, Brendan wanders back. He's looking thoughtful.

"It's out there," he says. "I've seen it. It's hovering around. I think it's waiting to see what we're going to do next. Isn't that interesting?"

I stare at him. No. That isn't interesting. In fact, it's the dead opposite of interesting. Not boring; just something I really wished he'd kept to himself. Marcus snorts in derision, and I agree with him, even if it is only to keep my mind on an even keel. Waiting to see what we're going to do, indeed.

"Yeah, right. I doubt that," Marcus says. "It's a dumb animal, Brendan – not some kind of malevolent force put in the lake with the prime function of fucking up our day. It's probably hunting or something."

Hunting, or something. Yeah. My stomach drops yet another notch. Thanks, Marcus. That makes me feel a whole lot better.

Fi rubs her hands briskly together.

"Well, we're ready. We'll use the rope, gather up a load of rocks – maybe some of those mussels as well, to add to the, ahh, chum mixture…" she pauses, and I'm glad she found that description as distasteful as I did. You know things have gone beyond desperate when you refer to one of your ex-colleagues as 'chum mixture'. In public, with other people listening to you. "So we can create as big a slick as possible. We don't need to attract it for too long – I reckon ten minutes tops – but even so, it'll be tight."

"So exactly how are we going to play this?" I ask. Not because I'm keen, but because I'm not prepared to be the one who takes the blame when this endeavour goes tits up.

"Well, I figure that I take my position at the water's edge – not in it, because I don't want my scent in the water until it is absolutely necessary. You guys then start chucking in rocks and slapping stuff around – you know, make a real commotion. Hopefully, that'll be enough to pique the creature's attention. If you see it, let me know. I can ready myself. Then on to phase two."

Ahh, yes. Phase two. I don't think any one needs to really detail that one, because we all know what that entails. Clark Chum.

"So…what are we going to do then?" I ask, as everyone else seems reluctant to ask. "Throw him in whole? Or…"

Look, okay. I know the answer. But I didn't really want to face it. I don't want to be the one who makes that decision. Call me squeamish.

"I think the answer is 'or'," Janos says. "A body whole will not produce enough of a scent trail to attract the beast. For that, you need blood. And… other things."

"Other things?" Marcus says, and screws up his nose. "Lovely."

"You've been diving with sharks, Marcus," Fi says. "You know what you have to do. I can't help – I can't get any of the scent on me. So it'll be up to you guys. I know it's pretty horrible – but this could be our only way of rescue. That's what's important. That's what you have to hold on to."

And that's how I found myself standing on top of a cliff, knife in hand, with a decomposing body at my feet.

Lovely.

Chapter Seven

The spot we've chosen isn't all that high, but it does have sheer sides that plunge into the frigid water below. Brendan tested the depth with the ropes, and it seems deep enough. We didn't think he'd found the bottom, but I find myself trusting him less and less as time goes on, so I'm not so sure. I don't really know what it is. He hasn't done anything, or really even said anything, but he has this faint smile plastered on his face that gets my back up.

Time to stop worrying about that. I have bigger, better things to occupy me. Like, how do you actually butcher a corpse? The way Janos and Marcus are hesitating, I don't think they know, either. I mean, it's not really an everyday skill that one picks up when leading a normal life.

In the distance, on the other side of the headland, Fi's kinetic torch blinks. We can yell – it's not far, and in the perpetual silence of this massive cave, sound travels well – but, for some reason, yelling feels wrong, so we're relying on lights.

The sequence of her blinks tells us she's ready, so I gather up an armful of rocks and hurl them as far as I can. They spatter into the still water, forming endless concentric rings, which ripple out and merge into each other. They are quickly destroyed by another barrage supplied by Marcus. Beside him, Janos throws the first of the weighted ropes in. It has been coated in mussel-juice, which we're hoping will help get the ball rolling.

Janos passes the rope to Brendan, who makes it dance a fandango. I throw in more rocks, and try to fight down the urge to giggle. This is fucking ridiculous. Maybe one day, I'll be able to look back at this and have a right good laugh about it.

I hear retching sounds behind me. It's Marcus, trying to hold it together. I can see why. Janos, with a look of utter disgust on his face, is in the process of trying to hack off Clark's leg at the knee. The smell is incredible and bile tickles the back of my throat. Finally, the joint gives way with a nasty sucking sound, and Janos ties the severed limb to the other rope. I force myself to swallow down my building nausea, because I know this isn't going to be the worst of it.

In the end, Marcus is the one who dangles Clark's leg over the edge. He's making these weird sort of wheezing sounds as he does it. Brendan glances over at him, but says nothing; just gives him that oddly irritating half-smile and then continues gazing over the water.

"Megan?" Janos says. His voice sounds thick. "Can you… can you give me a hand?"

Oh, this just gets better and better.

I look to Marcus, who is resolutely staring at the sea. And he's supposed to be the survivalist. I take in a couple of quick, deep breaths and face Janos.

"Sorry," he says. "But I can't do this alone."

No… he can't. And since I'm the only one left who isn't a pathological wuss or going seriously nuts, I feel like I don't have much of a choice. I stare down at the knife in my hand. It's quite big. A good four inches: a diving knife, given to me by one of the instructors. "For use in life or death situations," he said. Well, you don't get much more life or death than this.

I stand beside Janos and mutter, "Where's Yuri?"

Janos shakes his head. "I don't know. I hope far enough away, so he does not have to witness this."

He kneels down and begins running his knife around Clark's remaining limbs. He's used a bit of the stricken dinghy to cover Clark's face. I'm grateful for that. This is hard enough, without the thought of him staring at us.

I hack off a corner of the rubber to use as a makeshift bag. Using the same technique as before, Janos pulls off Clark's remaining limbs, one by one, the way a child might pull off the legs of a hapless spider. He goes to hand them to be, but I am too horrified at what I'm seeing to take them.

"Meg…" he says, softly, apologetically. I try to snap out of the hypnotic fugue watching him cut up Clark's body has put me under.

"Yeah?"

"You… you want to take those over? They will need to be… sliced. To let the, uh, attractant out."

The attractant. Is that even a word? But I know what he means. Oh, God, yes, I know and the thought turns me cold. I gather up my gruesome burden and zombie-walk back to the edge, where Marcus and Brendan are flailing their ropes around like lunatics.

"This is ridiculous," Marcus says through gritted teeth. "This is doing nothing – nothing at all."

"You're wrong," Brendan says. He's speaking quietly, but he may as well have shouted. "Look."

He pauses for a moment to point to a clear section of water, just out from the headland. At first, I see nothing, but then I catch the unmistakable churning of the waters as something large powers just below the surface.

My mouth dries.

"Do you… think that's it?" I ask.

Brendan gives me a complicated facial shrug.

He's right. How would he know? But it's our best indication that we've at least managed to attract something's attention. I wish again that the quality of the light were better, so we could have more of an idea as to what the hell is going on out there. Instead, I stoop down, uncover the slabs of putrefying meat that were once Clark's arms and legs and begin slicing them up.

The tip of the knife punctures the flesh a little more easily than I am comfortable with. The ensuing cuts don't bleed as such, but they do… ooze. A rancid congealed mess of black liquid spills over my blade and drips, like treacle, onto the patch of rubber that was once our boat. My stomach churns, and I start counting backwards. Anything to distract me.

Before long, I have a pool of viscous Clark chum, ready to empty into the water. Before I do, I glance over to where Fi is standing. She's poised, ready to dive. I don't know if I can really see that, or if my mind is painting the scene for me, but all of a sudden I feel the urge to run over and pull her back to stop her, to tell her no, it isn't worth it…

"It's here!" Marcus yells. "Go, Fi!"

He blinks his light, and she's gone. It's too late. I'm too late. I fling my rubber sheet out, keep hold of its edge so the chum splatters in the waters below. Janos is gesturing to me, his arms covered in gore. I haul the sheet back, my legs feeling jellified, and he dumps another load of matter. It's weird. Apart from breathing a little harder than usual, he seems okay, like he's done this a hundred times before. Me? I'm not so okay. This time, I can't help myself, and puke up all over the chum. It doesn't matter. It'll add to the piquancy of the dish. At least, I hope so.

I don't say anything, just wipe my mouth and drag the laden sheet back to the cliff edge. The sea is boiling below, as something big – no, scratch that, something *gargantuan* – writhes at the base of the cliff. I swallow hard, a stinging mix of bile and sweat, and heave the next load into the water. The only thing keeping me going is the thought that this might actually be working.

Beside me, Brendan and Marcus are flapping their ropes around as if St Vitus is in town. I peer back down, back down into the rolling blackness of the churning water below. No matter how hard I try, I can't make out the beast's true form; a glimpse of mottled hide here, the tip of a massive paddle there. Then, the creature bursts out of the water, its jaws open, ready to snap up anything in it's path, including me as I lean over more, slipping, tumbling, down into the red-black maw fringe with a battery of stalactite teeth…

I jerk back, my heart making a bid for escape through my ribs. I can't speak. I can't move. All I can do is stand and stare stupidly at the thing that has returned to the depths.

"Fucking hell…" someone manages to whisper. I don't know who it is. It could have been me.

"Meg! Meg!"

A voice, heavily accented, cuts through the hypnotic terror the beast below has put me under.

"It's huge," I whisper, and jerk around. "Huge."

I glance at the other two, and discover them both staring down, their eyes huge, their mouths slack.

"What did you say it might be?" Marcus manages to whisper.

"Pliosaur," I manage back.

"Fuck."

"Yeah."

"Meg!" It's Janos again, sounding even more desperate. "We need to keep it busy."

Finally, I gather enough of my wits to drag the remains of the dinghy back so he can fill them with the last of Clark's earthly remains. This time, I'm not sick. I don't even feel faintly nauseous. I'm too terrified for that.

"That's it," Janos says. "That's all we've got. It'd better be enough. Are you okay?"

I don't say anything. I can't.

This time, he helps me drag it back. Just as we approach the edge, both Marcus and Brendan let out dismayed shouts.

"No! Fuck… No! You… no, come on… Fi! Fi! Warn her! It's coming! IT'S COMING!"

Both Janos and I freeze. The rubber sheet splats to the floor, spilling its gruesome cargo.

What do they mean, it's coming? Janos breaks free first and runs to the edge.

"It's gone," he whispers.

I'm right behind him. And he's correct. The water, once a mass of churning foam, is calming. It has gone.

There is a final slapping sound as one of the ropes slides off and into the water. Brendan's. Marcus has thankfully hauled his in, but no one even thinks about congratulating him. We're all racing over to the other side of the headland, praying Fi had enough time to reach the shallows on the other side – the shallows where the monster can't follow. With something that almost approaches eagerness, I scan the opposite bank, looking for the tell-tale sign of her oblong headlamp.

There is nothing.

No light. No headlamp. No Fi.

I can't focus. I jerk my head around, searching, frantic, looking for something – anything – that indicates Fi is still out there, still our beacon of hope.

My heart leaps when I see a thin beam of light bobbing just above the surface. She hasn't got far to go now – fifty yards, if that. Go, Fi! Go! You can make it-

My elation freezes in its tracks. Just behind her, water swirls and the faint outline of something huge breaks the surface. It slides back down, quickly, deadly. We're going mental now, screaming, crying, begging her to move it, to get to the shallows, but we all know it is too late.

The pliosaur bursts from the water with a ferocity that stuns us all to silence. Fi is lost in a maelstrom of foam and mottled flesh. The only hint that she is there is her headlamp, which whips back and forth with frightening speed. She doesn't even get to scream before the pliosaur thumps back into the water, sending a wave rolling back towards us, like a final 'fuck you'.

It's gone. They've gone. She's gone. There's nothing left, apart from a rolling mass of water about fifty yards from the opposite shore.

Chapter Eight

We don't speak. We can't speak. All we can do is stare. Stare and despair.

Fi is gone. There's no other way of putting it. I think back to my split-second glimpse of that massive, crocodilian maw bursting out of the water to snatch the last earthly remains of Clark.

If only I hadn't paused. If only I'd managed to get the next load in. Maybe that would've given her the final few seconds she needed. If I'd been quicker. If only I'd-

Something heavy and foul smelling encircles my shoulders. Instinctively, I pull away, but it doesn't let me go. I look up. Janos is still staring out, over the water, his mouth fixed in a grim line. If it wasn't for the hint of moisture gathered at the corners of his eyes, I would have said he was angry.

I allow him to embrace me, but it does nothing to ease my sense of utter helplessness. I feel hollow. Dead inside. Our one, last hope has truly gone.

We stand motionless for what feels like an age. A snort breaks the moment, followed a giggle from my left.

Yuri.

I'd forgotten about him

"It swam up behind her, like a shark, and engulfed her whole," he says, holding his fist to his mouth. If anything, he looks even wilder now than he did before. "It got her. Like the dark. Like everything. It is their agent, their angel, their emissary…"

"Shut up," Janos says. He doesn't yell, but his message is clear. Shut up – or else.

"Whose emissary?" Brendan asks.

I could punch him. What the hell is he thinking? The last thing we need is to encourage the nutcase. Yuri grins and starts up that hyena-like laugh of his, and I find myself wanting to push him over the cliff.

"Them. Those who lie in the slumber, in between, in the spaces between spaces. They are still there, you know." He crashes forward, his movements jerky, his full attention upon Brendan. "They showed me. They showed me it all. Everything. What has happened, what will happen, and everything in between. Everything. Everything."

"For God's sake, don't encourage him!" Marcus snaps. Even by our standards, he is looking haggard. When Yuri grins at him and jabbers something inhuman, Marcus springs to his feet and marches over to him. Before any of us can stop him, he winds back his fist and punches Yuri squarely in the face.

That mobilises us. We all spring as one to pull Marcus back, because we know if we don't, he'll keep punching until there's nothing left. We know, because we feel the same way.

By the time we haul Marcus away, Yuri's nose is a bloodied mess. Not that it seems to bother him. He wipes the blood away and then spends a good five minutes staring at it, rubbing it between his fingers and smearing it over his knuckles.

I'm not too ashamed to admit that I'm wondering if it might be in our best interests to put an end to Yuri and his ramblings once and for all. But that makes me as bad – no, worse – than him, because he can't help being a nutter, whereas I have at least a shred of sanity, of reasoning, left inside me. At least, I think I do. I'm beginning to wonder. I mean, come on, I'm considering putting an obviously ill man out of his misery in front of multiple witnesses, so maybe I'm not so sane after all.

I close my eyes and take a deep, cleansing breath. In. Out. In. Out. In. Out.

"Megan? Are you okay?"

The question is tentative, as if the person asking is worried about something. I open my eyes and find everyone, minus Yuri, is watching me owlishly. I try to smile, but it falters on my lips. Why are they looking at me like that?

"You were… muttering," Marcus says. He looks apologetic. I don't know why.

"I was?"

"Yeah. Just a little bit."

"Oh."

I don't know what else to say.

Neither do the others, given that's where they drop it. Note to self – no more muttering. Even if I wasn't aware I was doing it.

"So, what now?" I ask, in an attempt at taking some initiative and at wiping the sympathetic looks off their faces.

Marcus looks away and Janos shakes his head. Brendan, rather worryingly, stares out to sea, imitating Yuri who has by now lost interest in his own blood.

"Come on, guys, we have to think of something-" I start, but Marcus interrupts me.

"What, like Fi did? You saw that thing. It… it… it *ate* her."

Thanks for reminding me, Marcus. Like I needed it. But instead of snapping back, I go for reasonable.

"I know. Her plan failed. So we have to come up with another one."

"Another one? Okay… so we're stuck on an island with no supplies apart from one length of rope, thanks to Brendan's inability to keep hold of his, some diving knives, the remains of a shredded, gore-covered dinghy and a resident nutcase who is GOING TO STOP FUCKING GIGGLING, OR I WILL STOP HIM!"

Yuri pauses his snorting as some kind of self-preservation instinct kicks in. He looks forlornly at us, and sinks to the floor, where he curls himself up into a ball. I exchange a look with Janos. We don't need to say anything. Forget Brendan. Hell, forget Yuri. We're going to have to watch Marcus from now on.

"I know… I know," I say. "It looks pretty hopeless, but there must be something. There must be. We can't just… give in."

"Oh no? We can't? Well, that's great, isn't it? Little Miss Optimism here is going to invent some kind of magic radio out of mussel shells and algae. What are you planning on doing, Janos? How about you, Brendan? You up for conquering Cold Fusion whilst we're at it-"

"Marcus, there is no need to be like that," Janos says.

"No need? No. Need?" Marcus explodes. "We are fucking *doomed.* Forget me ever seeing my wife again. Forget my kids. Forget ever being called Daddy again whilst they… whilst they…"

Marcus's voice dissolves into hiccups as tears stream unchecked down his face. It takes me a moment to realise I'm crying, too. Great big sobs, undisciplined and heart breaking rack his body as he mourns for his lost life, his lost family. I drift towards him, unaware I'm even walking, to try to comfort him, but he shoves me away. I stumble backwards, back to Janos, whose eyes are also red and watery. He blinks furiously as Marcus crumples to the floor.

"Come. There is nothing we can do for him. Give him is dignity, at least."

I allow Janos to draw me away.

"We're screwed, aren't we?" I mumble. I can't raise the energy to speak in any other way. "He's right, isn't he?"

Janos pinches the bridge of his nose. He has a good nose for a man, strong and long. I can't help notice the way his jaw clenches, defining it even more for a moment under his growth of messy beard. He'd look much better clean-shaven. Well… maybe not completely. A bit of stubble would enhance his rakish smile, the one he gives you when he thinks you've said something funny, which isn't often-

"Megan, I don't know what to suggest," he says, breaking the odd spell he cast over me. I mentally shake myself, ashamed that I'd even noticed these things whilst in this situation. What's wrong with me? We both look – and smell – terrible, and here I was, wondering what it might be like to explore that jaw and discover the lips that framed his seldom seen smile…

I wipe my mouth with my hand in an attempt at hiding my sudden discomfort. Maybe this was it. Maybe I really was on my way to doing a Full Yuri.

The water ripples again and something the rough size and shape of a sail breaks the surface.

A flipper.

It's as if the pliosaur knows our predicament and is flipping us off. Anger wells up inside me, smothering the confusing feelings of before.

"Fucker," I hiss.

"I know," says Janos. "If only we could convince it to leave. It's so… frustrating to be so close, yet so far."

So close, yet so far. Yep. That just about nails it.

***

We sit and mechanically choke down some raw shellfish. None of us feels much like eating, but we don't have much choice. It's either eat or die. It's that simple.

We're going to go back to the tower. Janos suggested it. It's going to be hard going, considering we only have one rope left now (and no one knows what to do with Yuri… but, then again, it's rapidly getting to the point where no one cares, either), but exploring the possibilities of that place is literally all we have now. You never know – maybe those tunnels might lead somewhere, away from this damned island and to a place where we might just be able to seek help.

Marcus is worryingly quiet. Ever since his breakdown, he's gone into himself. I don't like it. He might be a pain in the arse, but that's him – he's loud, he's rude and he's abrasive. One thing he's not is quiet. He says nothing when we dump the shells back in the shallows and collect water for desalination. There's silence when we enter the tower and set up the rope. It's like he's given up. Defeat now defines him.

As predicted, getting down the single rope is more of a struggle, but it's not impossible. Without a word, Marcus goes first, then me, then Brendan, and finally Janos. We leave Yuri outside – not that he'd enter the tower anyway. He baulked at going near it, and ran off when we entered. I don't know where he is, and quite frankly, I don't care.

Brendan takes the lead with obscene glee. He's all for it. Exploring this place is his everything now. He chatters on, speculating about its purpose and about who might have built it (aliens, naturally) and I wonder how on earth anyone ever took him seriously enough to award him his PhD.

Down we go, and with each step, my mood blackens.

Why the hell did I ever want to do this? We pass the room with the big windows, where we found Clark's body. Swimming back and forth are shoals of small fish, no larger than my palm. When they change position, they flicker silver, quite beautiful. I know then that if we had a way of getting back, I'd find this place as fascinating as Brendan. It is wondrous, but wonder is pointless when you can't get home. Wonder means nothing if it ultimately kills you.

We head down to the room with the chair.

Before we enter, we all agree – even Brendan – that no one is to touch it. Curiosity isn't going to kill these cats. No, that's the job of starvation and insanity- nope, shut up, brain. Not going there, remember? Time to try to find a way out of this situation. Hopefully. Hope. Abandon hope, all ye who –

I blink rapidly and grit my teeth. I have seriously got to get hold of myself.

Without the distraction of Yuri, it doesn't take us too long to discover something that resembles a kind of sash-like door. It is smooth and looks moulded into the wall, like a well-made blast door in an explosives lab. I have to hold in a laugh, because it's so science-fictiony, it's almost a cliché. There doesn't seem to be any particular way of opening it. Brendan gives us all a look I can only describe as apologetic, asks us to stand back and then starts slapping the doorframe and sections of the wall around it. When he hits a panel to the left, about a foot above his head, it blinks a dull red, and the door grates upwards. It stops halfway, clunking and sputtering.

"I'm not going under that," I say. "No way."

"There's nowhere else to go," Brendan says, ducking under.

Idiot.

"Brendan, what if it closes and we can't get out?"

"So what if it does? You want to go sit on the island and do the prehistoric equivalent of whale watching, then fine, you do that. Me? I'm going to explore and hopefully find a way home.". That's odd. I didn't expect that from him. Maybe his developing insanity isn't insanity at all, but rather optimism. Then again, plenty of people might equate the two. They do rather present themselves in similar ways.

Marcus ducks under the door following Brendan. He's not optimistic, that's for sure. Janos, however, hangs back with me. He runs a hand over his beard and frowns.

"We should find a way of propping it open. Just in case," he says. "Megan is right."

Megan is right! If my heart could sing, it would have – but instead, it only manages a little whistle. Megan is right. At last, someone is listening to me. I offer him a nod of thanks, but he doesn't return it. My heart shuts up and slinks back into the little pit of despair this place has created especially for it.

Brendan bends down so he can peer under the door at us.

"Find something, then. Oh, that's right… there isn't anything, is there? Or nothing you dare to touch, anyway." He disappears again. I hear a thumping sound, and the little panel glows red again. The door descends, jumping and jerking, until it is flush with the floor again.

"Brendan!" I snap, like a mother chastising a toddler who has just climbed a little too highly up the stairs. "Brendan! Open it!"

Before either Janos or I can slap the panel on our side, it again goes red, and the door chunters open. Again, Brendan bends down. He's grinning.

Bastard.

"Happy?"

No, I seethe inwardly. Not happy at all. But he's made his point, so Janos and I duck under the door and further into the complex.

Chapter Nine

"I think it was some kind of research station," Brendan says. We've been walking for a good few minutes now, down a corridor flanked by small rooms that contain nothing more than what looks like an elaborate chair. "This must be their rest area. I think these are their equivalent of bunks."

The ease in which he is hypothesising madness is really beginning to grate again, but none of us can dispute any of it, because none of us can come up with any better suggestions. When it comes down to it, this place is around one hundred and sixty million years old – no matter what is suggested, it's going to be madness, because whatever it is, it shouldn't exist. End of discussion.

"So, what were they researching?" I ask, or rather, snap.

"I dunno. Life? The Universe? Everything?" Brendan grins and I have to step back, away from him and the growing temptation to slap that stupid smile off his face.

Marcus, as silent as ever, is behind me. His face looks waxy, like a mask.

"You okay?" I offer him a nervous smile.

Nothing.

"Marcus…"

Nothing.

I sigh.

"We'll find a way."

I don't know why I said that, because I don't really believe it, but it gets a reaction at least. Marcus lifts his head, and I'm sure I see a ghost of a smile touch his lips. I don't know if that's because he believes me or pities me. I've decided I'm going to choose the former.

"Where's Janos?" Brendan asks.

That's a good question. I thought he was behind us, but he's not.

I pause before calling him. For some, stupid reason it feels almost sacrilegious to break the silence down here. The way the walls absorb the sound, deadening my voice, I think this place agrees with me.

Still no sign of Janos.

"Where the hell is he?" I ask. Brendan shrugs, and Marcus offers me a blank-faced stare. Little tendrils of doubt give my heart a warning squeeze.

First Nik, then Fi. Now Janos, too?

"Janos!" I call out again, fighting to keep the squeak out of my voice.

"He was behind us."

At last, Marcus speaks, but his voice sounds flat, like he's commenting on the weather, or the state of linoleum flooring. I don't think I've ever seen anyone so totally broken so quickly. I can't help but wonder how long it would take for that to happen to me… and if it's already starting. Bits of me that I once thought were solid are definitely fraying around the edges. How long before I unravel completely.

I nod quickly, and we begin to trace our steps, back down the corridor, peeking in each of the little rooms. I try to suppress the vision of Janos – good, dependable Janos – sitting rigid in one of those chairs, his face a rictus of terror, like Yuri's was when we found him.

Instead, we find him muttering to himself in a corner.

"Janos!" I don't even try to keep the relief out of my voice. "What are you doing? Why didn't you answer us?"

He spins around, and for a split second, looks… guilty? Seriously, that's the only way I can describe it. He clears his throat and offers us a grin.

"Just checking these nooks out," he says.

"Talking to yourself again, were you?" Marcus says, before I can answer. The two of them share a black stare, leaving me to wonder what had just happened.

"Yeah," Janos says. "It helps."

"First sign of madness, you know," Marcus says.

"I know, but it helps me retain information."

They continue to stare at one another, and I get the feeling that, should I step between them, I'd be vaporised.

"Okay… guys… At least we know everyone is okay," says Brendan. "Let's just keep going – and stick together, okay? No one needs to Scooby-Doo off. If you see something interesting, then just say so."

I'm impressed. That has to be the most coherent thing Brendan has said all day. Janos, however, doesn't seem to agree. At least, his body language doesn't. He stiffens, but then smiles, "All right. It makes sense."

And that's that.

I think.

I hope.

The corridor continues for quite a while, its walls a uniform grey in colour. Every few feet there's an archway, which leads into a small room with one of those chair-like constructions in the centre of it. Despite being empty for an unfathomably long time, no dust adorns the cold surfaces. In fact, there's nothing else except the chair. Nothing I could consider 'personal' can be found in any of the rooms. Maybe aliens don't have families. Or maybe they never got round to inventing photography. Or maybe I need to shut up now, because I'm beginning to sound like Brendan, and I don't want to sound like Brendan.

Finally, we are faced with another one of those blast doors. This one is open and the room beyond yawns wide, a great black hole where no light penetrates. Brendan fiddles with the wall, obviously looking for some kind of light switch, but comes up empty. At least he has the courtesy to look sheepish.

"Well, it was worth a try," he says.

As one, we step into the room beyond.

I can tell it's big. I can feel the space around me. The thin beams of our headlamps hardly penetrate the blackness, illuminating disjointed sections of huge structures that give away nothing and only add fuel to our already exhausted imaginations.

"What are they?" I breathe.

"I don't know," Janos replies.

No one else speaks, and silence reigns. The floor slopes down a little as we creep closer. Our headlamps pick out a curve here, a panel there. What looks like a girder spans the room just above head height. I make to duck under it, but I am stopped by an almost invisible wall made out of the same glass-like material, as the viewing window in the room above us. I peer through it and spy delicately fluted tubes that feed into it, snaking their way across the ceiling until they disappear into the darkness. The whole construction extends from floor to ceiling. I can only begin to imagine its purpose

"What would they want to keep in there?" Janos asks, and taps on the side.

"Dunno. Biological specimens?" Brendan sweeps his headlamp along its full length. "It's massive. Easily big enough for… you know."

Yeah, I know. I find myself nodding unconsciously, agreeing with Brendan.

"But why? Why would they want it in here?" I ask

"To study it?" Brendan offers.

"To study it…" I stroke my lips with one finger. Interesting. I wonder…

"What are you thinking, Meg?" Janos asks me. He's looking at me intently, which makes me feel like my clothes are about two sizes too small – no mean feat, since the suit is made to measure.

"I'm just wondering. If they did use this tank for biological study, how did they get it in here? There must be a way."

"You think we might be able to trap it in here?" Marcus asks, sounding a little more like his usual self.

"I don't know," I say. "But it's worth bearing in mind. If they did it, then there has to be a way…" I step closer to the slightly curved sides of the tank and peer in. I frown. That's odd. It isn't as easy to see into the depths of the tank as I thought it might be. There's some kind of strange distortion effect, like I'm trying to look through a layer of Vaseline.

Something akin to a ripple courses through the tank. My heart jolts, forcing me to take in a sharp breath, and I take a step back.

"What is it?" Janos asks.

I don't answer him, not immediately, because I'm not sure I believe what I saw. I run my hand over my face and try to ignore the way it trembles before gravitating back towards the glassy surface again.

"Megan?" I don't know who's questioning me, and I don't really care. The tank is again still, but I can't shake the feeling that all is not as it seems.

"What's wrong? There's nothing in there."

Whoever it is, they're wrong. I know they are. My physical senses might be telling me it is empty, but on a deep, instinctual level, I know the tank is anything but empty.

I can feel it.

Reality ripples again, and at the centre of the tank, a few bubbles form. That's the only way I can describe it – bubbles, suspended in the air. I sense someone standing next to me. They gasp.

"Did you see?"

I nod.

"What is it?"

I shake my head.

Brendan kneels beside me and peers closer. Whatever it is inside the tank ripples again.

"It's completely transparent," he whispers. "Like silica gel, only… purer." He lets out a low whistle. "What is it?"

Now Janos and Marcus join us. Both of them look pretty sceptical, like Brendan and I are sharing the same hallucination – and you know what? I might have believed we were, until they both gasp and confirm that they too can see the bubbles and the ripples.

"Wow," Marcus says.

We lapse back into silence, mesmerised. The bubbles multiply, catching the light from our headlamps, forming tiny rainbows within their hearts. I smile with wonderment, like a child. I don't think I've ever seen anything quite so beautiful in all my life. I tilt my head to one side as the bubbles begin to move around each other, through each other, melding and splitting like cells, forming new and ever more intricate patterns. They drift towards me, getting smaller and smaller until they smooth out, and I find myself looking at myself; my face, perfectly imitated.

I laugh.

The others crowd round me, but I'm not listening to their chatter. My liquid doppelgänger laughs with me, soundless, mimicking my every move. Entranced, I raise a hand to touch the glass. There is a note of alarm from behind me, but I'm not going to stop, not now. Whatever it is in the tank, it wants to communicate, that much is clear.

I touch the surface, and the transparent creature behind the glass forms a perfect replica of my hand in bubbles and rainbows. I pull it away and wave. It waves back. I know it's only copying, but I can't help but feel there is something more profound going on – after all, babies learn by copying.

"It's... you," Brendan murmurs. He leans over me, eager to create his own gel-replica. The creature in the tank does not disappoint. Within seconds, he too is staring at his own transparent doppelgänger, complete with awed expression.

"What *is* this stuff?" Marcus asks. "We shouldn't be fucking with this... I've got a bad feeling about it." I am momentarily shocked – and yes, annoyed – to hear such blasphemy. This 'stuff' is miraculous. Why must he be such an ass about everything?

I trace my finger in circles, and my mirror image traces them back. It is looking more and more like me, right down to the odd smattering of freckles that dusts my nose, each one picked out in tiny bubbles. The longer I watch, the more solid the image gets.

There is no other way to describe it. It's amazing.

"It's... it's like the perfect way to replicate things," Brendan says. He sounds awed. I know how he feels. "Why bother with cloning, when you could just get this stuff to copy it?"

That makes us all stop and think. It's all well and fine thinking of this stuff as a novelty, but Brendan is right – it must have a purpose. I think of the underground sea, so far from light, but so full of life.

"God jelly," I accidentally mutter out loud.

"God jelly?" Janos says. "What makes you say that?"

Just my luck. He had to pick up on that, didn't he?

"I was just thinking out loud. It's... it's nonsense."

"No... continue." I can see his reflection in the glass. He is looking intently at me, as if he can will me to speak. A small crease furrows my brow, and instantly, my doppelgänger copies me.

"We've been puzzling over the purpose of this place, who built it and all of that," I begin, slowly. "And then there's the lake. This far down, you'd think it would be dead – but it's not. It's teeming with life. Maybe…" I pause, aware of how ridiculous my suggestion might sound.

"Maybe?"

"Well, maybe this stuff has something to do with it? I know it's a lot to digest, and goes against everything I was ever taught about evolution and life on Earth. But what if – just what if – this is the answer to it all? What if they were creating life down here?"

No one says anything for a long while, leaving me wishing I had never opened my big mouth in the first place.

"So…" Marcus speaks first. He's looking pensive yet doubtful. "What you're saying is… this could be, like, God's laboratory?"

I shrug. Good old shrug. "Why not?"

"Because it's insanity, Meg. This isn't how life is created. You're a scientist – you know this!"

"I know… I know… and believe me, it sounds insane to me, too – but what other explanation is there?"

"Conquest." Janos says the word quietly, but it's like a drip of icy water down my back.

"Conquest? What do you mean?" I ask.

"I mean, they imitate us, they can take over."

"But humans weren't around one hundred and sixty million years ago."

It's his time to shrug. "Does it matter? We're here now."

That's an unpleasant thought.

"So… what? They pulled out a crystal ball and anticipated our evolution? Don't be stupid."

"I'm not being stupid. Think about it. Think about what Yuri said. 'I've seen everything; the past, the present, the future, all as one'. He said the beings who created this place live on the Outside – in the spaces between spaces. Our laws of physics, our dimensions, and yes, I am including time here, do not apply to them."

"But why us? Why humankind?" Marcus asks. "That's very humanocentric of you. Man always assumes, no matter what happens, that they are the ultimate goal. What if it isn't meant for us? What if… what if… they were hiding, or needed to… needed to… oh, I don't know, maybe this is all intended for whatever comes after us? Or maybe something is going on out there that we don't know anything about, and our discovering it is pure chance. Maybe we're insignificant, a fly in the cosmic ointment. That still doesn't answer what this stuff is, nor does it help us get off this fucking island, which is what we should be focusing on, not-"

"Uh, guys…"

Brendan interrupts us, sounding decidedly uneasy. I tear my attention away from my replica to find he has stood up. His mimic now has a body – and it isn't copying him. It's stretching up, reaching up towards the pipes. Two beams of light flash upwards. The top of the tank is a good ten or so feet up, way above our heads. I stand up, and my double does the same. It has a body now, just like Brendan's, and it too, is stretching up, becoming longer, more solid, more misshapen with each second.

"Shit!" I exclaim, and jump back.

My double doesn't. Instead, it keeps growing upwards, outwards, until it merges with Brendan's doppelgänger, twisting their forms together until they no longer resemble humans, but some kind of grotesque humanoid soup.

We should be running. We should be, but we aren't. We aren't, because we're transfixed, too horrified to even breathe. The oozing pile of limbs and eyes stretches up even further, its edges blurred and forever changing, until it reaches the top of the tank, where for a moment, its progression is halted whilst it splits, forcing itself into the tubes; tubes which run away from us, into the darkness.

One of us sighs. There is time. Time to escape-

With a sound like a shotgun, a thin, spidery crack radiates down from one of the pipes and quickly skitters downwards across the glass. Another one joins it, and the tank groans. The jelly within the tank pulsates, and the cracks multiply again. One of the tubes splits with an unpleasant, flesh-tearing sound. Droplets of gel, like blood from a scratch, ooze through these cracks, dripping down the surface of the tank, towards our feet.

"Holy sh- Run!"

No one needs to be told twice.

As one, we all turn and flee. We run back up the gantry, and just as we reach the malfunctioning door, the squeal of tortured glass gives way to a nerve-shattering crash.

We keep running.

One by one, we duck under the door and sprint down the corridor. We know we can close that door, but the sound of that shattering tank fills my mind. Will the door be enough to stop it?

Marcus dives under it first, followed by me, then Brendan and finally Janos. Janos slaps the panel and the door shudders to life, but it isn't fast enough.

"Oh, come on… come on!" I hear myself moan. In the distance, I can hear a schlepping noise, and my imagination obliges by supplying an accompanying image of that thing dragging itself along the floor with what looks for all the world like my arms.

"You have to hold it down," Janos pants. "Just run. I'm fast. I'll catch up."

"No," I say. "We'll do this together!"

"Fuck it, Meg – go on! We all need time to climb the rope – hopefully this door will stop it for long enough. Last thing we need is to wait by the ropes. I am a fast climber, and if you are all up top, you can help me. It is quicker this way,"

Marcus stares at him, and to my utmost surprise, nods.

"What? You can't be serious! We can't-"

"Yes, we can. We have to. It makes sense. Come on."

Without another word, he darts off.

Brendan gives Janos and me a wild look, and follows him.

"Go," Janos says. "Go with them."

The liquid sounds are now closer. The door is almost closed, but the gap is still big enough for the gel to squeeze through.

"I hate this," I say.

"So do I," Janos murmurs back. He reaches out with his free hand to touch my cheek. A furious lump bubbles up in my throat. This isn't fair. Why him? "You have to go now. I will catch up."

"And if you don't?"

He grins. "Then I'll give that gelatine bastard the worst indigestion ever. Now, run and do not look back."

He leans over and kisses my cheek. His stubble feels sharp against my skin. Then, realising I'm just about paralysed, he give me a little push. "Go! Now!"

And I do.

The rattling sound as the door slowly scissors shut decreases as I sprint away. It's amazing to think how long it took us to traverse the corridor first time around – now I make it in no more than five minutes. My lungs are screaming at me as I stagger up the ramp towards the Throne room, and my legs are already wobbling. I'm not unfit by any stretch of the imagination, but the strain of the last day (has it really only been a day? It feels like a decade) is taking its toll. Behind me, I hear footsteps, quick ones and that heartens me. It has to be Janos. The thought of something else mimicking him crosses my mind, but I push that away with each laboured pant. It's Janos. It has to be.

I push myself through the throne room and up the next section of ramped corridor. My throat is tight, my head light. I'm already exhausted, so how am I going to climb a rope at the end? Best not think of that. One foot in front of the other. Just keep going.

Below me, I hear the shriek of tortured metal. If I didn't know better, I'd say this place was in the process of collapse, but no, it's something far worse. A clang echoes through the complex as the door gives way. It is muffled through the layers of rock, but loud enough to make my heart skip and flood my system with a much needed burst of adrenaline.

It's through.

Oh please, oh please, oh please, let Janos be behind me. My mind gibbers like a stuck record, sending prayers up to a God I've never really believed in, but hoping if He is up there, He's as benevolent as the God Botherers say he is.

I'm all but staggering now, my breath coming out in short, agonising bursts. Past the viewing room. I don't even glance in there. The monster in the water could be staring right at me, and I wouldn't stop. Not when I am sure, I can hear the whispering schlub of something not quite solid, not quite liquid oozing its way up behind me.

Just a little way now and I'll be at the hole. I stumble. My legs protest as I try to maintain my balance. I bash into the wall, which feels freezing against my sweating body. It's hard to breathe now. My ribs are like steel, preventing my lungs from working. Every part of my body shrieks as I haul myself upright. My vision swims.

Must. Keep. Going.

The footsteps behind me (below me?) are closer now. Oh, *please* let that be Janos! I have to keep going. Who knows how close that thing is behind him. I have to clear the rope for him. I have to be out of the way. With each commandment, I drag my feel, bullying them into compliance. Run, damn you – *run*!

With gritted teeth, I force my body once again into action. Everyone has heard the phrase 'running for your life' – well, my friends, this is it. I'm running for my life. And it is agony.

The corridor opens up and my headlamp spies a thin piece of heaven dangling down, seemingly out of nothingness.

The rope.

The blessed rope.

It's moving in an awkward, jerking manner. Someone is still climbing it, but I can't wait. I have to start climbing, or I won't ever make it up there in time. I grab its flailing end and from above there is a grunt.

"Meg?"

It's Brendan. His voice is hoarse, exhausted.

"Yeah," I manage back. "I'm gonna… climb."

He doesn't protest, so I grasp onto the rope. My mind goes blank.

How do you climb a rope?

Oh, fucking hell! Meg – pull yourself together! You can do this! I batter down the adolescent me who always baulked at the prospect of rope climbing. Back then, it always seemed such an impossible task, but I've had years of training since then. Remember that. Always remember that. I haul myself up, grateful for the grip on my gloves – I am sure the rope would have slipped through my sweat-slicked hands if I didn't have them on - and grit my teeth against the collection of tiny supernovas that explode in my body. I wrap my legs around the rope, using by feet to grip the bottom, and slowly, I begin to drag myself up.

Two beams of light filter down, illuminating my way. I don't look up. I don't want to know how far I have to go. Instead, I concentrate on the simple task of hauling myself upwards. The rope jerks, and my exhausted limbs spasm. I slip, a fraction of an inch, and my heart skitters around my rib cage.

"Hold on!" I hear someone call from above. "We'll try to help!"

The rope jerks again, and I feel myself lift. Marcus and Brendan, who must be as exhausted as I am, are pulling the rope up. I risk a glance up. A disc of grey is cut against the infinite blackness.

The hole.

I'm closer to the top than I think.

Unchecked tears of relief fill my eyes.

I've made it.

But what about Janos?

I strain my hearing. There is nothing. Where is the thud of his boots? Any elation I felt at my imminent rescue flees.

"I… I can't hear Janos," I manage to pant as a pair of hands seizes the back of my suit and drag me upwards. I try to help them by grasping the edge of the hole, but my hands have seized up. The best I can do is force my knee up and help them lever me out.

"He'll be coming," Brendan pants. He rolls over, his face an ashen grey. Marcus is sitting next to him. Dark circles rim his eyes, and I can see the trembling of his limbs from here. He lets go of the rope, dropping it back into the hole. We cluster around it, lying on our bellies, listening, trying to hear something – anything – above the rasp of our own breathing.

Finally, we hear the exhausted slap of boots against rock. I can't do anything but grin. I look up – Brendan's grin mirrors mine, but Marcus looks less than happy. A monstrous urge to slap him rears up within me. How dare he? Janos has saved us! How can he look like that?

The rope jerks, pulling me out of my fury. Our headlamp beams are strong, but not quite strong enough to pierce the murk of the room below, so we can't see Janos, not yet.

"Hold on!" I croak, and take up the rope again. Brendan struggles to his feet and takes up a spot behind me. The rope is jiggling quite wildly, which make it hard to pull.

"Janos – be still," Brendan calls, or at least tries to. "Marcus?"

Marcus gives the hole one last look and then nods wearily. He joins us, and between all three of us, we pull.

The rope still whips around, making a hard job almost impossible.

"Janos," I say. "Keep still."

"It's coming!"

There is no mistaking the stark terror in Janos's exhausted voice.

It's coming. Two words we don't want to hear.

We pull by mutual agreement. Everything hurts, but still, we pull. Slowly, the rope is dragged up, its wriggling prize on the end. Now we can all hear it, a nasty, slithering sound, full of pops and burps and gurgles.

It's coming.

For a moment, I fancy I can hear words, unarticulated gibberish, amongst the slurping.

It's coming.

From the hole, a high-pitched shriek. We pull and pull and pull, until finally, Janos is within reach. He catches the edge of the hole and we scrabble at him, not caring what we grab onto, and pull him from the darkness. He is shaking, his eyes wild. Below, the light from my headlamp catches a glimpse of something huge not unlike a mass of bubbles, writhe.

The rope goes taut.

"Shit! Shit! Shit!" Brendan panics. "It's going to use the rope! It'll slither up! Cut it! Cut it!"

Marcus staggers to the ring, and with a swift yank, the knot that had tied us so securely unravels. It whips back, narrowly missing his face as it runs through the ring and snakes over the floor to disappear down the hole.

We are paralysed. Is that enough? Visions of it being able to climb the walls and ooze up through the hole, like sludge in a blocked drain, trip through my mind.

"We have to get out," I whisper. That's all I can manage.

No one argues with me.

As one, we stagger over to the entrance. There is a Three Stooges moment when we all try to fit through the doorway at once. We have no idea how to close it, since it disappeared the first time, and we are reduced to slapping the walls of the tower, desperately looking for the trigger mechanism. Just as I'm about to give up, Brendan lets out a whoop. I whip around, only to find the door has once again sealed itself. I don't know how we did it, and quite honestly, I don't care. All that matters is the thing is sealed in.

For now, anyway.

Chapter Ten

Silence reigns.

I don't think I could move, even if my life depended on it, which, ironically, it would do, if that door gives up the ghost. I don't have a clue if the bubble-thing (naff name, I know, but I'm too exhausted to think up anything else. So sue me) managed to get out of the hole, but I'm buggered if I'm going to go and look. By the looks of the others, they pretty much feel the same.

We're lying on the beach. Nowhere else to go now. The Tower is out of bounds and there's nothing else on the island left to explore. A depression has settled over us, a dark shroud that only allows us to breathe and hurt.

No one has said it, but we all know it.

We're dead.

***

I must have fallen asleep, because I don't remember anyone getting up. A sharp pain in my ribs brings me back to consciousness. I grunt and try to turn over, but the jabbing sensation won't stop. I open my eyes.

It's Yuri.

My heart jumps, and reflexively, I go to sit up. Every muscle complains. I hiss, as if that will help quell the fire within.

"You saw them, didn't you?"

The wildness in his eyes doesn't seem so out of place now. I expect we've probably all got a bit of that look to us now.

"I don't know," I say. "We saw something."

Yuri nods, nods over and over and over until I want to reach over and stop him, because watching him is making me feel sick.

"They made it," he whispers, and sidles up, uncomfortably close. "It's what they use. They take over worlds with it. Entire worlds. But it is dangerous. Very dangerous. Even to them. They made it, but it will rebel. Rebel against them. Then nothing will stop it. It eats and eats and eats until it consumes the world. I've seen. Seen it all.

I lean away from Yuri, but not because I don't believe him. I don't want to believe him, be sure of that, but it's becoming harder and harder to dismiss his ravings. What that says about my state of mind, I don't know. Should it worry me that Yuri is beginning to make some kind of horrible sense to me? Probably. Does it matter?

Probably not.

Not since we're all going to die down here.

I don't know where this sense of absolute certainty is coming from. I'd always considered myself something of an optimist. Now I'm not. Not now I've discovered you can't have a half full glass of anything without a glass.

Out in the depths, I hear a splashing sound. Oh, goody – our friend is back. All heads turn towards the sound, bathing the midnight water in torchlight. Just as the beams fade, a huge, whitish mound rolls.

Yeah, well fuck you too, monster.

Yuri leans in even closer. I shudder at his sudden proximity, but my shattered reflexes don't allow me to move backwards quickly enough before he can whisper in my ear.

"Don't trust him."

I freeze.

"What?"

"Don't trust him. He knows more than he lets on."

I frown. What the hell is he babbling on about? Who knows more?

Yuri nods once, gives me an odd, knowing look and scampers off, away from our makeshift camp, back into the unknown darkness.

He knows. Don't trust him.

Him.

One of three. Or none of three. There's no doubting Yuri's crazy. He's probably making it up.

But still.

Him?

One of three.

Roll the dice and make a choice.

I shake my head, as if that might dislodge the thought. A bolt of pain shoots down my neck and branches out, setting my shoulders ablaze. I wince. Don't do that. I can't think like that. We've been through so much together.

But still…

Funny how some seeds, once planted, just die, no matter what you do to nurture them. But others, usually the unwanted ones, the weeds, take root and grow. They not only grow, but they flourish.

One of three.

Take your pick, Meg.

My gaze travels from one to the other. First, Marcus, who is lying still, the crumpled photo of his family clutched to his chest. Then Brendan, who is doodling in the small traps of sand, and then to Janos…

Janos?

Where is he?

My heart thuds just once, hard enough to make me feel dizzy. We've lost so many recently. Have we lost one more?

Gingerly, I find my feet, my body full of pins and static. Two headlamps swing my way, but neither of their owners say anything. I think we're at that point now – that point where we simply do no know what to do. For now at least, I'm kind of grateful for it.

Now I'm up, I feel like I have the worst hangover ever. My head is pounding, my throat parched. I reach for my canister and wince at the warm, slightly salty water it contains. No matter how far technology goes, they never can get water treatment right.

I clamber up the rocks, my body cursing me with every step, and poke my head over the top. There, in the distance, is a pencil-thin beam that can only be Janos' headlamp. For some reason, that makes me feel better. It does strike me that maybe he's found a little hole to be alone, for whatever the reason, but I'm feeling selfish. We haven't spoken properly since I left him at the door, and the need to talk to him, to reason all of this out with him, is like a craving.

As I get closer, I hear a mutter. I stop. Voices? My first thought is Yuri, which sends a shudder down my spine. But no... Yuri is nowhere to be seen. I listen. It's coming from Janos.

I can't make out what he is saying – and chances are, I wouldn't understand him anyway, but by the pauses, I would say he's having a conversation. Which is nuts, because everyone he could be having a conversation with is either back at the camp or a stark-raving lunatic.

I don't know why, but suddenly my need to find Janos and talk to him falls away. I creep closer, careful to keep my body low. It feels kind of wrong, but I have to know who he is talking to.

I get close enough to make out words, and as predicted, don't understand any of it. But whatever it is, it sounds heated. He blows a deep, angry sigh and clenches his fists before saying one word I do understand.

"Shit."

"What's shit, Janos?" I ask.

He jumps. And I don't mean that figuratively – his body actually, physically jerks. He spins around, looking hunted.

"What?"

"I only asked what was shit. Who were you talking to?"

I was going to ask 'what were you saying?', but my mouth rearranged it. For some reason, Yuri's warning fights to the front of my mind.

Don't trust him.

Could he really mean Janos? A little ball of bile sits heavily in my chest, bitter and tight. I hate the way it makes me feel, but I can't help it. You can't help dread.

Janos grins, but it doesn't touch his eyes.

"Oh, Megan, it is you," he says. "No one. Just... myself."

"It sounded like you were arguing with someone," I say. Usually I would have let him get away with that, but a little bit healthy paranoia never did anyone any harm. I think.

Janos sighs heavily.

"Yes, it probably did. I am struggling, Meg. You know, with all of this." His shoulders slump and any feelings of dread flee. How could I doubt him? We all cope with things in our own way – this is obviously his.

"It's okay," I say. It's lame, but I don't know what else to say. I step closer to him, so I can touch his arm in what I hope is a comforting way. "We're all struggling with it. I mean... what now?"

From the way he swallows after that, I wish I'd never said it. Up until now, he'd always been the strong one – our rock (if you would pardon the expression), and to see him crumble... Yeah, that's hard.

It takes him a long minute before he tries to speak again.

"Do you know why I was hired?" he asks. I don't answer, just shrug. I know a rhetorical question when I am asked one. "I was hired to keep you all alive. I am an experienced caver and extreme environmental expert. This should have been easy. But now Nik and Fi are dead, Marcus is half-crazed with grief, Brendan... well, I do not quite know what is going on with Brendan, but it worries me, and then you..."

"...And me, what?" I ask, after he trails off.

"...And you... each time I look at you, I see nothing but trust and despair. Despair at our situation, and trust in me." He stops to wipe his hand over his mouth. It makes a rasping sound. "And I don't know how much longer I can bear to see that. Or, indeed, face the day when there is only despair left."

My throat tightens at his stark admission. Salt gathers behind my eyes. I don't want to cry, but I don't think I can help it. I'm hungry, tired and frightened – and so is he. In one movement, I move closer to him and wrap my arms around him. I feel his heartbeat accelerate, and it takes him a few seconds to respond, but when he hugs me back, it is a bone-crusher. That's when the tears fall, and there's nothing I can do to stop them. They come from every single part of me, wash through me, gathering bits of emotional crud and specks of terror, cleansing me as I sob into Janos's chest. I feel pressure on my head, and it takes me a few seconds to work out it is Janos, stroking my hair.

"What are we going to do?" I manage between hiccups.

"I don't know," he whispers.

We stand in that dark and alien place, holding one another. We do not speak. We cannot speak. Once my tears subside, I raise a hand to wipe my face – I'm not exactly a pretty crier, and I know my eyes are swollen, my face puffy and red, but that doesn't seem to bother Janos. When I turn my head back, he catches my cheek with one hand. No words are exchanged, but I know exactly what he intends to do, and I have no problems with it at all.

In the past, I have been guarded with my kisses. I ration them, because I think they are special. Not because I think I'm special, of course – a drunken Christmas snog happens to me as much as the next woman – but the real, sincere ones… those I don't dole out often, because they inevitably lead to choices I do not want to make.

Down here, those choices mean sweet F.A.

There is a selfishness to his kisses; a hunger that has less to do with desire and more to do with the cannibalistic need to prove that he is still alive. I know, because I feel it too. It doesn't matter who we are, where we are, what we are. Right now, we are reduced to two entities, joined.

A distant splash brings me to my senses. A sour taste fills my mouth, bringing with it the scent of dried sweat and fear. The switch is flicked, and what felt so right now feels all together wrong. Whether it's because he senses my reluctance to go further, or because he himself feels the same way, I don't know. That sudden hunger now satiated, we release one another. Awkwardness fills the space between us. Was that a good idea? I don't know, and I don't think he knows either.

A flicker of movement behind him catches my eye. I allow my gaze to slide towards it. Right on the edge of my vision, a figure crouches. It waves at me and takes one sidling step closer. It is Yuri. He is staring at me with an intensity that is frightening, and when our eyes lock, he shakes his head and points at Janos.

Before I can react, he slides back into the darkness.

Chapter Eleven

I don't know what to think.

Was Yuri really hinting what I think he was hinting? Not that I can ask him. I can't find him. None of us can. He's found a hidey-hole somewhere, and he's not letting on as to where it is.

I wish I had a hidey-hole.

A hidey-hole where I could curl up into a ball and try to forget any of this ever happened. A hidey-hole with a bed, and a thick blanket that I could pull up over my head to keep the monsters out. Just like home.

I wish I were home.

I've tried not to think about it, but it's getting impossible not to. Once upon a time I viewed home as an anchor, as something tying me down. This trip was supposed to be the once-in-a-lifetime opportunity that allowed me to break free of home's mundane shackles. And the ironic thing? It is. Once in a lifetime. Never to be done again.

Because I can't see there ever being a chance to live any other kind of life.

This, my friend, is it.

The water is gently lapping at the base of the cliff. Yep, the same cliff where we 'buried' Clark. It's almost inviting. If I peer down, I can just about make out the tiny waves. I wonder what does that? The tides on the surface are governed by the moon, but I can't see how that would be much of an influence down here.

The moon. I miss you. Funny how you take things for granted. I had the chance to just sit and stare, taking in its beauty, so many times, but didn't. Probably because I'd always thought it would be there, waiting for me.

Not any more.

The faint phosphorescence of the chemotrophic bacteria filming the rocks makes the water glow. It's beautiful in its own way, I suppose.

I don't want to be here any more.

There. I've said it.

I pick up a stone and weigh it in one hand. Is our friend out there? The one that is so desperate for us to stay? A plume of fury boils within me. That thing. That monster. Everything is all its fault. Why did it attack the boat? Why? I wind my arm back and fling the stone as hard as I can. As soon as it leaves my hand it may as well be invisible, the only proof of its existence a faint 'plop' as it strikes the water's surface. I don't even get to see the ripples. Suddenly, I feel a lot like that stone. I was once in someone's hand, solid and true, but then I was flung into this dark hell… and then what? I sink. Down, down, into the depths, where no one will find me – just a few invisible ripples to mark my existence on this planet briefly.

I want to go home. The fury twitches to a longing so acute, I actually think something vital within me is fit to burst.

I catch a glimpse of white, out on the water. A strange sound, like someone opening a fizzed-up beer follows.

It's him. Her. It. Whatever.

Our keeper. Our doom. Our Great White Whale.

Funny, we spent so much time speculating what it was at first. Now, no one says anything. Probably because it doesn't matter. A positive identification won't change anything. Naming it won't allow us to control it, or tame it. If anything, we should name it 'master' and have done with it.

It sinks below the strange waves, only to surface again, closer to me. It's almost as if it knows I'm here.

Here, alone.

Here, waiting.

***

We suffer another meagre meal of raw shellfish before any of us dare broach the taboo subject of 'what next'. Despite our reluctance, it has to be done. We can't continue sitting on the rocks, brooding indefinitely. We need to do something, even if it is just to admit we don't know what to do next.

Brendan is sitting near me, looking like he is listening. I wish he wouldn't. I think I prefer the air of tired defeat on Marcus's face to the almost eager alertness in his. It's unnatural.

"Can you hear it?" he says. Marcus's eyes swivel slowly from him to me, and then off into the distance. He doesn't need to say anything for me to agree with him.

"Hear what?" I ask, more to humour Brendan that anything else. "The creature in the water?"

"No. No... below us. Underneath. It's slithering around, trying to find a way out." He's grinning again, and now I understand that it's his way of dealing with it. He's not amused. He's terrified.

Before I can answer, Janos lets out a short, explosive sigh and stands up. He doesn't look at any of us as he stalks away, but we watch him. Marcus shakes his head, and I go back to picking at my fingernails.

"Do you think Janos heard it?"

"No, Brendan, I don't," I hiss between clenched teeth. The fury is back, and right now, it wants to take Brendan's head off. His constant questions, that grin, his... his... 'oddness' has gotten to the point where it isn't so much grating as eating away at me, like acid, and I don't know how much more of it I can take. "Will you just shut up for once?"

"I only asked..."

"Meg has a point," Marcus says. He sounds so tired. Once upon a time, he would've been the one snapping, but it's as if he's had every ounce of stuffing knocked out of him. "Time to be quiet."

Brendan nods, a quick, jerky movement, and the fury is replaced by shame. He's frightened. I'm frightened. We're all frightened. I shouldn't snap. So I try to humour him.

"What do you think it was?" I ask. "Down there."

Marcus gives me a hard look. I know, I know... you defended me and now I'm all but encouraging him. My bad.

"I don't know," Brendan says. "I don't think I've ever seen anything like it before. I… I don't think it's meant to be here. I mean – not now. Not ever."

"What do you mean by that?" I ask.

"He means it's not indigenous to this planet." Janos's voice floats out of the darkness. "That they brought it with them."

Brendan's eyes widen as if in shock and nods. I don't think he can quite believe that Janos has come to the same conclusion as him. I know I can't. I swivel around to address the gloom behind me.

"So you're all for this being some kind of alien entity too?" I try not to sound sarcastic, but it's hard, given the topic of the conversation.

"After all you've seen…" Brendan says, sounding incredulous. "Meg, why do you insist on not believing?"

Good question.

"Because… because it's madness," I say. "I mean the supposed pliosaur in the water? That's hard enough to swallow. A one hundred and sixty million year old species, surviving underground into modern times? It's the stuff of late night movies and Loch Ness nutcasery. But I've seen it, and so I can't deny it. It's there. If it wasn't, I'd be gone."

"Then why do you deny the thing in the tower? You've seen it, clearer than you've seen the pliosaur. Why is that so hard to admit to?" Brendan asks, and for the first time I hear a note of true anger in his voice. Stupid thing is, after listening to myself, I don't blame him.

"I… I don't know. Because it's insane. I mean, I know this whole situation is insane, but at least it's, I don't know… 'earthbound' insanity. A prehistoric monster, surviving in the depths of the earth? Rare, but not unheard of. Look at the Coelacanth, or the Megamouth. Both prehistoric relics, thought to be extinct but actually flourishing in a new environment. Like I said – unlikely, but not without precedent. But that…that *thing* in the tower? There is no precedent. There is literally nothing like it on Earth."

"Well… maybe not literally, Meg." Brendan is now looking thoughtful, and a new surge of worry piles on top of the old ones.

"No… no. Bren – don't try to tell me there's something like that in the fossil record that has just happened to survive down here-"

"No, Meg, nothing like that," Brendan interrupts me with a dismissive wave. Glad to know he's not that far gone. "I was thinking more of what it might be constructed from." He pauses, gathering his thoughts. No one interrupts him. "It seems to be gelatinous by nature, and mimicked us, yes? To me, that doesn't say animal. More like colony."

"Colony? What the fuck are you on?" Marcus says. "Coral reefs are colonies, but you don't see them taking the form of the fish around them."

"Of course not. I still stand by my assessment that there is no analogous species on earth for what lives down there, and there never has been. But I do wonder if it's not one life-form, which is where the colony comes from."

Little pathways light up in my brain. I can see where he is coming from. I don't want to, but it does make a horrible kind of sense to me.

"Like a hive," I say.

"Well… not really," Brendan says. With each preposterous idea, he is becoming more and more coherent. I'm not sure if that says more about him or more about my mental state, but I can't deny that I'm intrigued.

"Think of siphonophores," he continues. "Tiny individuals that make up, and control, a whole. Maybe even the bridge between a true colony, like a reef, and multicellular life."

"Excuse me," Marcus interjects. "Siphono-what?"

"Portuguese man o'war," I say.

"They're jellyfish."

"No… they're not. People think they are, but they're actually colonies of simple individual animals that form a whole organism."

I can't believe I didn't see this. I know I'm a geologist and therefore my biological knowledge is pretty sparse, but this is beginner level stuff. Brendan is now making a kind of horrible sense.

"Indeed," Brendan says. "Lots of tiny organisms behaving as one."

"But that doesn't explain why it mimicked us," I say, grasping at any straws or remaining sanity.

"No, you're right – it doesn't. A Portuguese man o'war floats around until prey becomes entangled in its tentacles and it feeds. And who knows? Maybe, in its own environment, that's exactly what this thing does. But it's not in its own environment – I hope – so it has evolved strategies. Or, at least, it involved strategies with some help."

Janos, who has been silent this whole time, now looks up and fixes Brendan with a hard stare.

"So… what you're saying is that this… colony has evolved mimicking as a way to entrap prey?"

Brendan shrugs. "Why not. Look at the amount of species out there that use mimicry already for that exact purpose. Bioluminescent lures in anglerfish. The tongue of the alligator snapping turtle. Spiders in general. It's a tried and tested strategy.'

"So? What are you saying, Brendan?" Marcus asks. I never thought I'd ever be happy to hear that special brand of angry sarcasm he relies on so much, but what do you know? I am. It makes him sound more like himself. "How does that help us? How does that get us off this fucking island?"

Brendan stops short, licks his lips and shakes his head.

"I… I don't know, Marcus. It's just interesting-"

"No, it fucking isn't interesting. It's useless. How long have we just spent going through this shit, when we could have been thinking about more important things, like… like…"

It's like the switch is flipped again, and the once gloriously angry Marcus folds in on himself, literally and figuratively. Yes – we could have spent the last ten minutes discussing our predicament… but to what end? That we're well and truly fucked?

Or are we?

My mind keeps replaying the whole notion of mimicry, like a video stuck in a loop. My face coalescing in the slime. It copying me. It attacking. Mimicry. Mimicry. Mimicry.

"What is it, Meg?"

Janos's voice is soft, as if he doesn't want to break my train of thought.

"I don't know. Just something. Or nothing. Or… something."

"Megan?" Marcus looks at me, frowning. "Are you okay?"

I look down and realise I'm wringing my hands a little too much. I force them apart and clutch hold of the rock I am sitting on.

"Yeah... I was just thinking. I mean, I think… I wonder… I…"

Do I really know what I'm thinking? Mimicry. That's what I keep coming back to.

Mimicry.

"Tell us," Janos says. "It can hardly be the worst thing we've heard in the last day or so."

That's true. I take in a deep breath and frown, trying to bully the amorphous feelings into some kind of coherent idea.

"Mimicry," I say. There. It's out now. "It mimics things, right? To lure prey. Or, at least, that's how it looks. So what if…" I pause. Am I really going to suggest this? I take another deep breath and let it out slowly. "What if we could use that to our advantage? Who knows how long it's been trapped down there, laying dormant, hungry. All we have to do is point it in the right direction of some really impressive prey."

I haven't said it outright, and judging by the frowns, it's taking them a little while to get their heads around what I am suggesting. Hell, it's taken me long enough, and I'm the one who came up with it. One by one, the frowns melt away and eyes swivel towards the water.

"If you're suggesting what I think you're suggesting…?"

"Yeah. I know. But it might be our only chance. Apart from climbing across the ceiling, we've tried everything else."

"But that means freeing it," Brendan can't disguise the horror in his voice at that. My stomach tightens and convulses. I know how he feels.

"Freeing it?" Marcus chips in. "Why the fuck would we want to do that?"

"So it can get into the water and – hopefully – devour the pliosaur."

Janos speaks in such a matter-of-fact way, you'd think he was making suggestions for a shopping list. But he's right. That's about the gist of it.

"And what then?" Brendan asks.

"We use the time to escape." I say, as if it's the simplest thing in the world. "The distance to the opposite shore isn't that far – like Fi said, we could get across in five, ten minutes, tops."

"And if it doesn't work?" Brendan continues to needle me. Since when did he decide to grow some sanity?

"I don't know," I admit. "But I don't see any of you making any other suggestions."

"We're not making them because we're trying to think of something that doesn't come with a 99% certainty of death!" Marcus says.

"Oh, so what? We stay here? Do that and we've got a 100% chance of death, Marcus."

"There could be a rescue group on their way as we speak."

"There could be," I admit. "You could be right. There could be a rescue group currently navigating the flattener right now. Then what would they do? Stand on the shoreline and wave at us? Because unless they're packing some heavy-duty explosives – which they won't, considering we're in a fucking cave environment – how the bloody hell are they going to get past the pliosaur? Remember, we were supposedly a rescue group, and look at the stand-up job we did." I shake my head, almost unable to believe this is me talking. "No. If we're going to get out of this alive, we have to be the ones who get ourselves past that monster and off this island. And the only way I can think of stopping that thing is to throw something bigger and more dangerous at it."

Marcus shakes his head and blows out a furious sigh. "I can't believe this. I can't believe you. You, of all people! And what happens to this thing once you've let it out and it's done its job? Say it does work. Say we do manage to convince it to indulge in a monster dinner rather than a human one. What's to stop it following us? What's to stop it from reaching the surface? Can you imagine what it could do?"

That stops me short. I'll admit, I hadn't thought about that. And Marcus is, of course, right. Bringing that thing back with us would be disastrous. Who knows what terror it could unleash? My shoulders slump forward, and tears ignite the back of my throat. So much for that.

"Don't be disheartened," Brendan says. He goes to touch my shoulder, but I throw off his hand with a violent shrug. Disheartened? Fucking understatement. I want to scream, but I can't trust my voice, can't trust myself; I know no words would come out of my mouth, just huge sobs, and for some reason, that really bothers me. I don't like crying in front of others at the best of times, and I'm not going to start now. So, rather than stay there and risk it, I whirl around and run. I don't know where I'm going. I just let me feet take me wherever.

No one follows me.

Chapter Twelve

With a bit of hindsight, maybe my idea was a bit flawed, but the fact that no one else had anything else to suggest means it still stands.

I've calmed down a bit now. The others have kept their distance, which is good, I think.

I'm near the tower. It's not much of a dash to get from here to the shore. I'm sure we could make it. My main problem is I'm not sure how we would coax the damn thing out without it engulfing one of us, if that's what it does.

I wonder if it only looks like what it mimics, or whether it has a rudimentary sentience. Being able to bargain with it would be the easiest way out of this, but that's not going to happen. Even if it is intelligent, who's to say that intelligence is anything like ours? For all we know, that… stuff is what was behind this place. Maybe it… they… oh, I don't know. Whatever. Stick to the singular. It's easier that way. So… did 'it' build this place? Is 'it' responsible for Yuri's state of mind?

I wish we had a load of explosives. Then we could just set a charge under the viewing window and 'kaboom' - instant access to the sea. Except that wouldn't work, not really. For all we know, we wouldn't make it to the viewing window in the first place. Anyway, if we had access to explosives, we would have blown that motherfucker out there in the water up the moment we realised it was there. Boom bang baby – you ain't trappin' me on no island.

I'm gibbering again, aren't I? I can't help it. The darkness out there is finally seeping in here. I can feel it. It's like damp. It rises. Rises through you until there's no light left.

Oh, sweet Jesus – ouch. I've been gnawing on my nails again, and I just caught one on the nap of my suit. That's definitely seen better days. We've only been down here… how long? A day? Two? A week? I don't know. There's no way to mark the passage of time, no sun to rely on, no passage of day and night to count. I remember when someone – was it Marcus? I can't remember – speculated that two weeks was too short a time to go completely doolally, but I'm not so sure now. We haven't been down here that long, and I'm already beginning to feel the cracks in my mind split and widen.

Is that all it takes?

How long before one of us finally cracks completely?

A soft tap on my shoulder jump starts my heart and sends me skyward. I would have cried out if my throat were capable of screaming that high a note.

"Come. Come. Come with me."

It's Yuri again. Now my shock plummets and crystallises in my stomach as pure, primal fear. There's something about the way he is looking at me that makes my skin want to slough off my body and crawl away. I shrink back.

"What?"

His eyes are wide and staring, unblinking, inhuman.

"Come. Come and see." He tugs at my arm like a small, demented child.

"See what?" I manage to ask.

"To see what he knows. I told you. He knows more than he lets on. Come."

He gives my arm one last tug, and then he scampers off into the darkness. I have no idea how he can see. He doesn't have a lamp, but that doesn't seem to hamper him any more. Maybe his… experience in that chair has fundamentally messed with not only his mind, but his body too.

"Come," I can hear him whisper from the darkness ahead of me.

I have my belt knife. I draw it as surreptitiously as I can whilst I stand up and palm the blade so Yuri won't see it. I creep forwards, following his voice, using the light from my headlamp to stop myself from tripping over any stray rocks. He's there, waiting for me, crouching by a large boulder. He shakes his head at my approach.

"No, no, no, no, no… turn it off. No lights. He'll spot us if you wear a light. Off. Off. Off."

Off? What? I go to ask him if he's totally gone insane, but I stop myself. Stupid question. When I get close enough, he reaches up and before I can stop him, he snaps my headlamp off.

My little world is plunged into blackness. The crystal of fear in my belly shatters, and sprouts thorny tendrils of panic that seed throughout my system. One false move from Yuri is all it will take. Just one ill-judged touch and I know I will plunge this knife into whatever I can find. Then I shall go completely and quite emphatically mad.

I don't know if Yuri senses this, or if he's just giving my eyes time to adjust to the total absence of artificial light, but gradually, as they do so, the panic ebbs. It doesn't go away completely, but it ducks just far enough below the surface to allow me to operate on a kind of rational level. I don't put my knife away, though. Oh no. One false move from Yuri, and he's dead. Simple as that.

The faint phosphorescent glow of the bacteria-covered rocks only really gives the shadows an edge, so walking is difficult. I twist my ankle on one particularly evil stone, and let out a bark of pain. Yuri turns around, fingers to his lips, shushing me, his eyes pleading. I test my weight on my foot. Pain flares, but it's not enough to stop me. Thank goodness.

Yuri slows and places a hand on my forearm. He crouches, pulling me down with him. My hand tightens around the hilt of my knife, but it's okay – he only wants me to follow him again, but this time, I have to do it as slowly and as stealthily as I can.

It isn't long before I spy a beam of blessed light up ahead. Every now and again, it moves, side to side, up and down, sometimes slowly, sometimes fast. It's a headlamp, and whoever is wearing it is quite agitated.

Yuri stops behind a boulder and gestures for me to peek over the top. Before I do, he gives me one, last, desperate look and raises a finger to his lips in the universal gesture for keep quiet.

I inch up over the cold damp stone and squint ahead of me. Janos is standing in a small clearing, surrounded by a litter of stones. He is talking quietly, but judging by the way he keeps throwing up his arms and shaking his head, he's upset about something.

I watch, the growing sense of unease in my belly coming to a simmering point. This isn't normal, talking to yourself stuff. I don't need to understand what he is saying – the pauses in his tirade tells me this is a two-way conversation.

But a two-way conversation with whom? Himself? If it is, then he's more far-gone than I ever thought. The way he hisses and splutters when he talks speaks of a fury only another person could provoke, which can only mean one thing.

He is talking to someone else.

Someone else.

Someone not here.

Someone who could save us.

The unease boils over and solidifies into pure, white-hot rage. We've spent the last God-knows how long down here, trying to survive, trying to think of a way out… Fi's death… unleashing that… that thing in the tower – all of it purposeless. All of it stupidity. All of it worthless.

Because Janos has a radio.

How the fuck did he manage it? My fists curl even tighter, but now my knife is not for Yuri, it is for Janos, the man I trusted, the man I desired, the man I thought was on our, on my, side.

It was all a lie.

"I told you," Yuri breathes directly into my ear, and then backs away and melts into the darkness beyond.

I slide back down the boulder. There are no butterflies of doubt in my stomach, no jitters to unsteady my hand. Fury has galvanised me, like steel. I am solid. I sneak closer, keeping low to the ground, all my attention on the traitor amongst us whilst Fi waves at me before diving into the frigid depths within the confines of my head.

He did nothing to stop her. All this time, he had the means for our rescue, and he kept it to himself.

Bastard.

I cut towards his light. I could just sneak up to him in the dark and stick a knife between his shoulder blades, but I don't want to do that. I want answers.

I pause, just so I can hear what he is saying. To my surprise, he is now speaking English, so I can understand every word. Such is his arrogance.

"No!" he is saying. The light wavers again as he shakes his head. "You cannot. It is not fair, not right, not…"

"What isn't right, Janos?" I ask from the sanctuary of the shadows.

Janos's head jerks up and his hand snaps down from his ear. So that's it. A microtranceiver. He must have had one on him the whole time, but our radio array is on the other side of the strait, which means he has an independent frequency.

So this was all planned.

"Megan!" he all but barks. His mouth flaps open and shut, like a land-bound goldfish. "M-Megan…"

"I asked you a question, Janos. What isn't right?"

He pauses and shifts uncomfortably. Then his expression hardens to display a rock-hard determination. I have seen that look before, and for a fleeting moment, the steel within me trembles. Over the last few days, I had softened towards him, almost forgetting that he was a man with whom you did not trifle. The simple fact that he was the one in the wrong was the only thing that stopped me crumbling completely under that stare. He was wrong. Simple as that.

"You do not need to worry about that," he all but snaps.

I take a step towards him, my knife clutched in a way that means it wouldn't be immediately noticeable from his perspective.

"Oh, I think I do," I say. I'm surprised my voice sounds so even. "Talking to yourself. I can't believe I fell for that one. How long have you been in contact with them, Janos?"

He swallows and his eyes flicker to one side. It's only a small crack in his granite façade, but it's enough for me to work with.

"We trusted you," I continue. "I trusted you. Out of everyone on this team, you were the one I thought was the most dependable…the most solid. But no. It's just a lie, isn't it? You were never one of us."

"Megan," he begins, but by now my fury is up again and I want to hurt him, hurt him badly, as much as he has hurt me, hurt all of us with his lies. I stride over to him, forgetting that he has extensive military training and pull the knife forward, just under his chin. For all of you out there wondering if you could do it, actually take a blade and plunge it into another human being, let me tell you this. Yes. Yes, you would. If you're as furious, as broken, as disappointed as me, you could.

The moment the knife's tip grazed his neck, I thought Janos would bat it away and put me into some kind of headlock – or worse, snap my neck to keep me quiet. But he doesn't. Instead, he keeps staring at me, looking curiously defeated.

"I did not want it to be this way," he whispers.

"You didn't want... what? What the fuck does that mean?" I hiss, too angry to shout. "You've got a radio! You've been feeding back! Fi didn't need to die! We didn't need to sit in desperation, wondering how the hell we'd get out of this alive. She didn't need to sacrifice herself, because you..." I jab the knife up. It nicks the soft skin under his chin, and a little bead of blood forms there, "had a radio all the time, but you never stopped her. You never once said no..."

"And you think that is because I am some kind of cold-hearted bastard?" he says, sounding remarkably calm for a man with a knife held to his throat. "Megan... have you ever once stopped to ask yourself why they sent an unknown geologist, a washed-up biologist with a shaky history of mental illness and a bunch of adrenaline junkies down here, when they could have sent a crack military team?"

I allow my knife to drop a fraction of an inch. What? What did he mean?

"Yes, I can see it. You're beginning to question it. Killing me gets you nowhere. We are no rescue team. We are here for one purpose and one purpose only."

"And what's that?" I manage to whisper.

"They needed... guinea pigs."

"Guinea pigs? For what?"

He sighs and closes his eyes in resignation.

"Ask yourself – are you really the best person out there to be involved in the rescue of an experienced team of cavers? Come on. Before this, your experience of caving was restricted to pottering around in safe environments – Karst limestone complexes that already had their insides mapped and routes secured. Then, you're approached about this. Sure, you're already on the team, but only as a scientific adviser. Why send you down? Really, I am asking. Why did they send you down?"

"Because… because I'm a geologist. A sedimentologist – Karst limestone is my speciality, but I've been working on shale beds for some time now, looking for shale gas. That's where the money is. That's what they pay me for. To find gas."

"Ah yes, to find gas. Much gas down here?"

"Well, yeah… until we broke through and discovered this environment. Look – I asked to be involved. Any geologist would. This is the closest thing we'd ever come to a true prehistoric environment, short of inventing a time machine. I had to be involved…"

I trail off. The disbelieving, almost pitying, look on his face says 'nice try, kid – wanna know the truth now?' I drop my hand containing the knife completely. What's the point?

"You had to be involved. For science. Indeed. And, for the main part, what you think is the truth, is the truth. Things changed once they starting probing this new environment. Discovering the space… that was easy enough. What they didn't expect was the signal."

"The… signal?"

"Yes. A strange, pulsing signal, too regular to be anything natural. They wanted to find out what it was, so they sent Alpha team. All military. I was supposed to be with them, but a minor injury kept me out of it. As it happens, it was a rather fortuitous sequence of events for the company. You see… the footage did not just stop. Alpha team did not disappear without a trace. They knew what had happened to them. They saw it all, including the creature in the tank. That is their true interest."

"Their…true…what?" My world suddenly feels very heavy. My head swims, and for a moment, it feels like the floor is made of blancmange.

"Think of the money they could make if they could figure out what that substance could really do. Each and any militarised country in the world would pay literally anything to have something like that at its disposal."

"But why us? Why send another team, under false pretences? If they knew all along what happened to Alpha team...why send us? Why?"

"Why, indeed. Think about it. Why send faceless people, people the world may not miss too much, into certain danger, and almost certain death?"

My stomach flips over. I swallow hard to keep the bile from rising.

"Test subjects," I say. "They wanted us to see what that thing could do."

"Exactly. They have footage of the discovery of the substance, and the subsequent deaths of their crack-team... but that wasn't enough. They needed to know that wasn't a fluke. This complex is largely unexplored. Rather than send in anyone important, why not ask if people want to go? Or better yet, get them to volunteer, or in your case, demand."

"Why are you here, if you know all of this? Why come? They've sent us down here as some kind of experiment... Why you? You didn't need to come."

"Because I have no choice. They needed someone to relay back information. Unfortunately, they did not bank on giant prehistoric marine reptiles living in the water, and so I lost all my camera equipment. The only thing that survived was my microtranceiver. That's it."

"So, what does that mean? We're being left down here?"

"No, Megan. It actually means the opposite. They are coming."

"Coming? To rescue us?" As soon as the question leaves my lips, I know it is a stupid one. Of course, this isn't a rescue mission. Why grow compassion and altruism now? Janos shakes his head, all the same.

"No, not a rescue mission. They cannot risk this getting out. Civilians are a risk. They do not have the training on keeping their mouths shut."

Janos' expression has changed again. This time, no amount of fury in the world is going to protect me. I take a step back, away from him.

"I see," is all I can say before I turn tail and run.

Chapter Thirteen

I can't believe he didn't leap after me and snap my neck there and then. Maybe he wasn't expecting me to just bolt off like that, without a light to guide me – or him. Or maybe he doesn't want to be the one who silences me. Because they are coming. The company is sending in reinforcements, not to rescue us, but to kill us.

I have to get back and warn the others. That's all I can think of now. Warn them, and keep them safe.

Because they are coming.

They might even be here.

That sends a jolt of panic through me. I'm keeping low, trying to scramble down to our makeshift camp as quietly as I can, but every footfall sounds like a gunshot, every stone I dislodge an avalanche.

I still can't believe Janos hasn't found me. He's supposed to be an expert, isn't he? So why isn't he after me like a hound after a hare? No. No. I can't think like this. I have to get to the others. Back to the others to warn them.

The glow from the rocks is hardly enough to navigate by, but I don't dare turn my headlamp on. I reckon I'm getting closer – the bioluminescence is getting stronger, which means I am getting closer to the water's edge. I think I hear a clattering from behind me, which sends my heart off on a merry jaunt around my body. I freeze and hit the deck, listening.

Nothing. Nothing but the pounding of my blood in my ears.

Still, I listen.

And listen.

The darkness settles over me like a shroud. I try to calm my breathing, slow my heart, and listen. Forever listening.

The faint sound of rippling water against rock is all I can hear. Maybe it was just my imagination after all. But I know better. Every sense is screaming at me, every instinct wired.

He's nearby.

A soft, slithering sound to my right. Someone moving stealthily, their bodysuit dragging over the top of a boulder. Is that Janos? Well, who else could it be? Apart from Yuri, of course.

The thought does not comfort me.

I hold my breath. My eyes pulse heavily in their sockets. The slithering noise stops. Seconds that feels like minutes that in turn feel like millennia inch by. My face is hot, my lungs burning, but I dare not breathe.

The slithering starts up again and disappears. Although I want to let my breath go in one explosive sigh, I ease it out, painfully, silently. The slithering does not return.

I ease myself off the floor, millimetre by millimetre, until I manage to tuck my feet under me. The sound of water came from up ahead, so I creep that way. My senses are singing now, and I realise I have never felt so alive. The irony is not lost on me.

Staying low, I pick my way carefully over a ridge of boulders. I peek over, and a small sob escapes me. Down below, just the other side of this ridge, I can see two figures sitting, their headlamps dimmed by their lack of activity.

Brendan and Marcus.

They're still alive.

I scramble over the ridge and slide down the other side, sending a cascade of debris down with me. I don't care if Janos hears me now. I've found the others. Between us, we'll restrain him, but before that, I have to warn them.

Their heads snap around at the sound of my descent. One of them stands up and wanders over to me, looking blissfully unaware of the danger he might be in. In a way, I'm thankful for that. Shame I am the one who has to break it to them, really.

"Meg?"

It's Marcus. I stagger to my feet and try to tell him everything I have learned, but it comes out as a jumble of heaving sobs and disjointed words. He takes my hand and helps me find my balance, asking me if I'm okay, what happened. It's okay - but it's not okay, it's not okay at all. I want to scream at him to shut up, but I simply can't find the breath for it. My head feels about eight times too big and my ribs are squeezing me like a vice, making it harder and harder for me to concentrate. Marcus catches my cheeks between his hands and demands that I breathe with him, in and out, in and out, and slowly the pressure eases. I try to speak, but he shakes his head and continues the breathing and I have no choice but to comply with his instructions. In and out. In and out. In and out.

"Jesus, Meg," he says eventually. "You're in a right state. What's happened?"

Now it's my chance. I open my mouth… and my brain shuts down. I have so much to tell him, but no idea where to begin.

"Megan?"

"It's Janos," I start. "He's not what he seems to be. We're in danger – big danger. We're… guinea pigs, for some kind of experiment, or something. I'm not quite sure I understand it fully, but they knew that thing was there, Marcus. They knew, and they sent us to see what it would do."

"Hey, whoa – slow down," Marcus says. "What are you on about? What's this about Janos? And who knew what? You're not making sense."

I clutch onto Marcus's arms, staring right at him, willing him to understand me.

"We're not supposed to survive," I say.

By the look that crosses his face, I can tell he still doesn't understand me, but before I can continue, someone shouts out. I jump back, heart pounding, head singing before I realise it isn't Janos, but Brendan. He's jumping up and down, waving his arms in the air, shouting, "We're here!" I snap my head up, and from across the strait, I see what he saw – the bright lights of headlamps, shining in the distance.

It's too late. They're here.

I go to run forward, clamp my hand around Brendan's mouth and drag him to the floor, but before I can move, there is a soft 'thht' noise. Brendan staggers back, and then crashes to the floor.

I don't have to tell Marcus to get down. "Turn your light off!" I whisper, and scuttle towards Brendan. He is lying on his back, eyes staring, with what looks for all the world like the end of a crossbow bolt protruding from his forehead.

"What the fuck?" Marcus whispers.

I extend a shaking hand and press two fingers against the side of Brendan's neck, even though it is blatantly obvious to me, he is dead.

"What the fuck?" Marcus repeats. I turn to him, shush him and then slink back to the line of boulders.

On the opposite bank, the clean up team have erected huge floodlights, which illuminate the strait in all its subterranean glory. Now I can see the majestic stalactites that hang down from the ceiling hundreds of feet above, each one a gigantic sword of Damocles over our heads. The water itself sparkles, and the rocks glisten. Voices float over the water. I don't understand what they're saying, but I don't need to. It's obvious what they're doing.

They're looking for us.

Brendan's corpse is momentarily illuminated, his blood a black slick on the rocks. My breath catches in my throat. He thought we were finally saved. How wrong he was.

"Why did they shoot him?" Marcus asks. It's a simple enough question, but one with a very complicated answer, an answer I'm not sure I can give.

"Because he was in the wrong place at the wrong time," I reply.

"Just as both of you are," a voice whispers behind us.

Janos.

I whip around, my knife ready. He is crouching a few feet away, his hands raised.

"Believe me, if I wanted you dead, I would have snapped both your necks by now," he says. "As it happens, I am in as much danger as you are."

"Oh, yeah, right," I say. 'They're here to get you out and clean up the rest of us."

"That was initially the plan, yes," Janos interrupts. "That plan has now changed. I was supposed to do the 'cleaning up' before they arrived. I refused. Now they'll clean me up, too."

"Clean you up?" Marcus asks, obviously confused. "Will someone please tell me what they hell is going on?"

Janos glances towards him, and then back to me.

"We do not have the time right now," he says. "Megan, you're going to have to trust me."

"Trust you?" I spit. "Trust you? Fuck off, Janos. I wouldn't trust you as far as I could throw you, not after all this –"

"All of what?" Marcus asks plaintively.

"Mr Macho is a mole," I say. "We were sent down here as guinea pigs, as expendables, to find out more about that thing in the tank. He knew. He's been reporting back to whoever is really in charge of this operation all the time. Now they're here, and they need to shut us up. Terminally."

Marcus's eyes widen.

"You bastard!" he hisses. "You mean… Fi… she didn't need to die?"

"No. He had a microtranceiver all this time."

"They knew we were stranded?"

I go to answer, but Marcus waves his hand to silence me.

"I want to hear it from him."

Janos sighs and hangs his head. "Yes. They knew. I told them. But I need to straighten a few things out. Yes, you were all sent because you were deemed expendable – but I had no orders to kill any of you. I was told to keep my role top secret. No matter what happened, I was to tell no one. You were all to believe I was simply here as part of the team. No, Megan, that's the truth. Please, don't roll your eyes at me. The kill switch order came after the thing in the tank escaped. That is what they're after, and they can't risk a leak. But I refused. Therefore, I am now a problem too. A problem that will need cleaning up. Please. I know you have no reason to believe this, coming from me, but it is the truth."

The floodlights sweep past us again, and we all duck reflexively, even though the boulder line covers us completely. Marcus shakes his head and swears under his breath.

"Okay. So what now?"

I feel the back of my neck prickle as my hackles raise. Is he…Is he *believing* him?

"Marcus? You don't really believe any of that."

"Meg, what choice do we have? He's right – he's had plenty of opportunity to kill us, and hasn't. We stick together and we've got a higher chance of getting out of this."

"Oh yeah, right, and exactly how are we going to do that?"

Janos shuffles a little closer to us, and I am forced to squash down the instinct to lash out at him.

"I have been thinking about that," he says. "And I might have an answer. Not a good one, but it's something. They know about the pliosaur and the other prehistoric inhabitants of this strait, so they know they have to overcome that to get to us, and their prize. They also know using ballistic weaponry and explosives down here would be suicide, which means they're going to have to stop that thing the old fashioned way."

The old fashioned way. Despite all the damage it has done to us, the thought of them killing that majestic creature just because it stands in between them and something they want sickens me. Sure, – so we'd have done the same if it meant we could've found a way home, but that was for survival's sake. Killing because you want something that is not vital to the continuation of your life… that feels wrong to me.

"So, what? They'll find a way over here. So, what?"

"I have been ruminating on your former idea, Megan," Janos says. "You suggested luring the thing out to devour the pliosaur, thus allowing us to swim across in relative safety. The problem with that was how we do lure it out? Well, now we have an added complication, or maybe not. Let them deal with the pliosaur. Then lure them to the colony's lair. They only have Alpha team's footage of the place, and my commentary. They don't know where the thing is."

"Yeah, but the problem with that is neither do we," I say. "If we go down there, what's to say it won't kill us first?"

"That is always a risk, but we have the edge. We know what it looks like, and more importantly, what it sounds and smells like. They don't. Our chances of using its instincts against it are greater than theirs. They want to use it as a weapon? Then why can't we?

"Janos… that's insane. Sounds like you're trying to lure us down there to finish off what you started," Marcus says, and I have to admit, he has a very good point.

Janos runs a hand over his head and sighs.

"I cannot make you believe me, much less trust me. All I can say is I will be with you. If this was purely a chance to dispatch both of you, why would I do that?"

From the other beach, there is a click and a low hum starts up. Janos jerks his head up and frowns.

"What is it?" I ask.

"I don't know…" he replies.

We peek over the top of the boulders. Across the water, people are preparing to launch a rubber dinghy similar to the one we had, only this one has something rectangular and black strapped to its side. I frown and glance at Janos, then Marcus. There bewildered looks answer my unspoken question – they don't know what it is, either.

We watch, mesmerised, as they push the boat into the shallows. Four of them board. From here, I can see they carry what can only be described as state-of-the-art crossbows. It makes sense. No guns down here – too risky. The fact that they're carrying them now kind of drives it all home, even more than Brendan's murder.

They're here to kill us.

Part of me wants to withdraw, get the hell out and find a place to hide, but another part wants to witness what happens next. I have no idea how they are going to overcome the problem of the pliosaur in the water, but my curiosity gets the better of me. I'm guessing it has something to do with that black box, but I could be wrong.

The boat is about halfway across the strait when the now familiar ripples on the surface of the water start up. The pliosaur is there, circling them judging by the pattern the ripples make, but not attacking. The hum kicks up a notch, and I feel my teeth rattle. I wince. Whatever that thing is, it might be keeping the pliosaur at bay, but it also risks bringing the cave down on us. Someone obviously comes to the same conclusion, because it gets turned down again.

"They're using low frequency sounds to deter it," Janos mutters. "Simple, but seemingly effective. Also a gamble. Unfortunately, one that seems to have paid off for now."

The ripples back off, and a huge flipper flicks out of the water. Again, I am stunned by the sheer size of it. It dwarfs the dinghy. As if out of frustration, the pliosaur slaps it down onto the surface, sending a wake of wavelets towards the little boat, making it buck and dance. A shout rings out, but the pliosaur keeps its distance.

They're three-quarters of the way over now.

Time, as they say, for action.

Chapter Fourteen

The way back to the tower was difficult without lights, but not impossible. The bioluminescent glow of the bacteria helped, but not as much as the floodlights. It looks like they brought at least one across, because the light available suddenly intensified, sending my heart rate skyrocketing.

They're here. They made it across.

Luckily, the base of the tower isn't visible from the landing point, so we don't have to bother with hiding. We're not bothering to hide our tracks, either. We want them to follow us.

We all pause at the base of the tower. I lick my lips. They're rough and taste of salt. I don't know why, but this gets me wondering just how much of a mess I look, which is ridiculous. I'm hanging onto my sanity by the skin of my teeth, just about to put my life on the line… and part of me is worrying I might not be looking my best.

I hear Marcus swallow audibly like they do in the cartoons. Janos lays his hands on the stone and pushes. As before, the wall melts away, leaving a hole. All three of us take an involuntary step back.

Nothing but darkness wafts from the room. Behind us, in the distance, we hear a shout. That's enough to bolster all of our nerves. Together, we step inside. I sniff tentatively, but that faint metallic, almost briny smell is not present. We risk turning our headlamps on, because even with the aid of the distant floodlight, it's still as black as sin in here.

Everything looks just as we left it.

Well, everything apart from the coils of rope next to the hole in the ground.

We glance at one another. We all know the rope was untied, but none of us want to think about how it ended back up here. I'm reluctant to touch it, and by the way Marcus backs off, I would say he's thinking the same thing I am. In the end, Janos picks it up, ties it off and lowers it down into the hole. No one speaks. When it is done, Janos nods to us and starts to climb down. I run my hands down over my thighs, as if I can dry my palms through my gloves and for a moment, I'm not sure whether my trembling body will let me climb the rope properly. Taking in a few deep breaths doesn't seem to help, either. I screw up my face and force my hands to flex, gripping the rope as tightly as I can. Then, before I get a chance to change my mind, I slither off the edge to hang just below the surface of the hole. Now all I can do is concentrate on the simple act of climbing down, one hand over the other, using my legs to balance me, until a pair of hands grasps me from below. I bite back a shriek. I know it's only Janos, but my nerves are in shreds. He helps me untangle myself from the rope and find the floor. I know I have to help Marcus now, but my attention snaps to every corner of the room, looking for movement, straining my ears to catch the slightest sound. I refocus back on the rope, which is wriggling back and forth like a noose on hanging day. It seems to take Marcus an age to clamber down, even though in reality, it probably took mere seconds.

Now all three of us are down, we turn as one to regard the opening to the corridor and the rooms beyond.

No one has to say it, but I know we're all thinking it.

Where is the colony?

"We must stick together," Janos says, as if it isn't stating the bloody obvious. Marcus offers a tight nod. Me? I just continue to stare into the abyss ahead.

As we knew he would, Janos takes point. It occurs to me that I know little of his background, but it is obvious from his stance and the way he is holding his hands that he has a military background and is used to carrying a weapon. He doesn't creep around, he's stalks, like he owns this place. If he thinks that lends him an air of confidence, he's wrong. It just makes him look arrogant.

We descend in silence, pausing every so often to listen and to smell. Each time, there is nothing. What the fuck is going on here? I don't understand. I thought it would be waiting for us, waiting to pounce the moment we dared set foot in its domain again, but it's as if it was never here. A horrible thought steals over me. What if it isn't here? What if... what if we'd had some kind of group hallucination? But then, why would the Company be here, ready to kill us so they could take possession of whatever it was? Another thought creeps up on me, even more insidious and unpleasant than the last one. How did we even know the Company was out to kill us? After all, we only had Janos' word.

And Janos was the last person to leave the tower.

The last person?

Or the last... thing?

By now, my heart is clanging in my ears, my breath straining my lungs. I'm close to panicking again, and I have to stop it, but I don't know how. The conspiracy of Janos not being Janos at all, but instead a construct of the sentient alien colony sent up to lure us back into its web, whilst our rescuers search vainly for us on the surface won't go away. I feel hot, so hot, and amorphous black blobs dance before my eyes. Before I can pass out, my mind throws me a wild card – Brendan's blank, blood soaked face.

Brendan's blank, blood-soaked dead face.

They killed him. Not the colony, not Janos, but them. The Company. All he did was wave and yell. And they killed him.

It's enough to allow my breathing to loosen and my mind to clear, just a little bit, enough to allow me to concentrate on my surroundings.

We're now in the doorway of the first room. For the first time, things are different. The room is lit, and some of the panels have lights upon them, which blink every now and again. Strange characters spider their way across the panels. I can only guess that they are some kind of language. The viewing window is open, and the sea beyond it teems with life thought to be long extinct. I want to marvel, but I'm too scared, too worried to take it all in. Instead, we skulk through the room, past where we found Clark, inspecting the terminals as we go.

Someone has woken this place up, and it wasn't us.

"It's not here," Janos says. "Come on – we have to go deeper."

Something that has been niggling at me for some time wriggles its way forward. I frown.

"What is it, Meg?" Marcus asks.

"I don't know," I say. "Just that…if the colony was…trapped in that tank, then what attacked Alpha team? It couldn't have been that. That can't be what the Company is after…"

"That's because it isn't."

The answer comes from a far corner. We all jump at it, and Janos snaps up an imaginary gun.

A figure uncurls itself from the corner and stands up.

It's Yuri.

Funny, I'd forgotten all about him.

"What do you mean?" I ask, trying to keep the tremor out of my voice. "What are they after?"

"I told you, they showed me. Showed me everything. But I didn't want to be shown. Not after what happened to Clark. They made me and they filmed it." He pointed to Janos. "He knows. He saw. There was one in the chair. One. Translucent. Part of the collective. The only bit that escaped. In the…in the tank." He spins round, his arms thrown wide. "What was left of them. Their consciousness all decayed, all insane. The last one entered me to use my body to escape, but human minds are not meant to do what it wanted to do. We are pure matter. They are not. Many as one, infecting each other, unable to transfer, so they fester, fester together, fester as one…"

Behind him, the shadows grow. A faint smell of metal and brine ripples towards us. I can't feel my body as my mind reels back, away from the gelatinous monster that looms over Yuri. It is grotesque, yet beautiful, glistening and perfect. Upon its surface, faces appear: mine and Brendan's. They smile, just as we had smiled at it in the tank. The smiles droop to form leers, and the colony slurps forward. All the while, Yuri's expression of pure ecstasy never changes. The doppelgänger's faces split and dissolve away as the blob slithers over his body, engulfing him until he is wearing it as a shimmering second skin. It lifts him up, and a thin whine escapes him as his body deflates, as if something vital has been extracted. The whining stops, and there is a sickening sound of tearing. The transparency of its body does nothing to hide the horror as the colony tears Yuri apart, allowing his body to sink through it to the floor, whilst his head is pushed forward until it is extended upon a neck of slime.

"You come here to destroy us?"

There's no trace of Yuri's voice left now. What is left has a strange, choral quality to it, like a hundred voices speaking in unison, giving it a metallic edge. The colony stretches up, a glistening wall that towers over us. There is no escape; no way that we could ever run and survive. I shake my head, half to dispute its assertion, half to try and clear the pounding.

"We have survived aeons. You are but a blip – an accident of evolution with ideas above your station."

I work my mouth, knowing this may be our only chance at survival, but the words won't come. The surface of the colony ripples again, subtly shifting its bulk closer to us. My heart, already pounding, feels fit to burst.

"That may be," I manage to whisper. "But we're not here to destroy you. Not us. Not the three before you. We just want to go home. We're trapped -"

'Trapped?" The colony withdraws just a fraction of an inch, as if in confusion.

"Yes," I say, diving for the one common thread we have. "Trapped. All we wish to do is escape. Go home. Nothing else."

The colony pulses, and Yuri's face is sucked back into its body. Now there is no pretence at language, no common form of communication. The whole entity shudders and surges forward without warning.

***

Where am I?

Wait… What is I?

'I' is…

'I' is…

Light, bright and white. Then colours, so violent they hurt. A blast of cold against wet skin.

This is 'I'.

There's nothing I can hide. Nowhere to escape to. It inhabits every part of me, every fibre of my being, sorting through my memories as a researcher tears through old records. It is too much. Pain beyond pain as I am forced to relive every moment of my life – every triumph, every failure, every pleasure, every agony – everything all at once. Just as I think I cannot take any more, that I will explode from the overload of sensation, it withdraws.

Something cold strikes my cheek. It takes me a moment to realise it's the floor. I have collapsed, or so it seems. Or maybe I was dropped. I don't know.

My head is killing me. It thumps as it hurries to re-order my memories, to prioritise, to re-bury. I can't stop shivering. I try, but it's pointless. Every part of me trembles, recovering from the invasion of my being, my consciousness, my soul.

I have no idea how long I lay there, shivering, desperately trying to figure out who I am again. It could be seconds; it could be hours.

Time means nothing, a human construct, a useless conceit of our species' importance. That is the one overriding sense I am left with. Time is meaningless. Time is nothing.

Finally, I manage to blink and open my eyes. It takes a moment for me to remember how to focus. When I do, no concerned faces stare back. Just a wall of translucent matter that undulates with every beat of my heart.

I am left with one certainty.

It believes me.

I haul myself up to my knees. Both Marcus and Janos are staring at me, a blank, wide-eyed horror staining their faces. Should the colony decide to judge them next… well, let's just hope they leave Janos alone.

Nothing is left of Yuri now. Of that, I am sure. I'm not even all that sure the person we recovered from the chair was Yuri at all now – I wonder if he was more colony than human. A buzzing sensation at the base of my skull reverberates through my body, telling me I'm right. He saw too much, too soon and it fragmented his human consciousness. But lessons have been learned, and that won't happen again.

I hear the faint but rhythmic tread of stealthy boots upon stone. I whip my head around to the source.

"Someone is coming."

Are they the ones?

"Yes," I say.

"Yes, what?" Marcus asks. He sounds hoarse, like he is in need of a stiff drink.

"Nothing," I reply. They don't need to know.

The colony glides forward, past me. Marcus and Janos plaster themselves up against the wall. They're terrified. I can smell it rolling off them in waves. They needn't worry. They're not the targets.

"M… Megan?" Janos asks.

I say nothing. I don't need to. Instead, a smile curls my lips, and I follow the colony down the corridor.

Chapter Fifteen

It's amazing how quiet you can be when you know how. I creep down the corridors, keeping to the walls. Marcus and Janos are some ways behind me, but I still wince each time they move. Amateurs.

I can hear movement from up above. I wait for a moment, just to check that all the clean-up team have descended and are now in the corridors. The last thing I need is for one to escape up the rope.

The colony is all but invisible, clinging to the ceiling, waiting. I flatten myself against the wall and do the same. Not long now.

The red pencil-thin beam of a scope-light sweeps the corridor ahead. They're not taking any chances. I'm not really sure why I worried so much about their intentions. They're no match for us, not now. No, now they are the ones who should be worrying. They just don't know it yet.

I sense another set of footsteps behind me, and I turn my head just enough so I can mouth stop whilst raising one hand. Janos and Marcus do not question me. Something deep within them, some animal instinct, knows better than that. Instead, they copy me, folding themselves into the ridges of the walls.

The clean-up team are close enough for me to identify them individually. There are four of them, four skittering hearts that belies their steady hands. They're frightened.

Good. They should be.

Another scope follows the first. Interesting. No headlamps or flashlights. Not that it matters. Night vision isn't going to help here, no matter how sophisticated the technology. There is a faint slurping from up above – the colony drips down long, thin pseudopods of matter that sways despite there being no breeze, not so much to ensnare, but more to warn the mother organism. I'm not sure exactly how it senses the world, but I do know it has no need for sight, smell, or sound, despite it speaking through Yuri to me. That was entirely for my benefit. Judging its hunting method, it lives in a world of touch a world of vibration and sensation.

We wait.

My breathing is steady. For the first time since I landed on this godforsaken island, I actually feel...calm. I shouldn't, and part of me knows this. It runs around my body, looking for loose threads to tug at and unravel my resolve. Finding none, it slinks back and gives up.

A black clad figure turns the corner. I keep perfectly still. He should be able to see me – after all, my body heat must be like a beacon in the night, but he doesn't react. Whether it's because he's too busy sweeping the walls to notice me, or it's something else, something innate to me now, I don't know. He inches forward in a half crouch, military style, bearing a kind of high-tech crossbow as a soldier would carry an M4, ready to shoot at the slightest provocation. He flinches ever so slightly when the tendrils of mucus touch his cheek, and raises a hand to bat them away.

Then he screams.

It echoes throughout the complex, summoning his friends. Eager to aid their comrade, they are quicker, less cautious than they might have been, allowing the colony to ensnare another of their number before it detaches itself from its hiding place and engulfs them whole.

The scream is cut off. It reverberates in the air for a mere fraction of a second afterwards, but to me, it feels like an age as I watch it ricochet off the walls, a wave of crackling energy that lessens with each surface it strikes.

The two helpless members of the clean up team are now plastered to the floor, almost as if they've been shrink-wrapped. I raise a hand to stifle the urge to giggle. They look so surprised. They thought they were the predators down here – how wrong can you be? The colony constricts again, forcing themselves into the very pores of the men, splitting skin and rupturing organs. The men can't move, can't make a sound as the colony seeps into them, invading every part of them until they turn to mush, mere nourishment for the collective. There isn't even a bloodstain to tell where they had once been. All that is left is a shredded uniform and their weapons.

As the colony regroups, I wander over and pick up one of the crossbows. It looks easy enough to use. Small yet wickedly sharp bolts are loaded in a cartridge that protrudes from the stock, with a high-tensile string that you just pull back when you've fired, allowing another bolt to slide into the chamber. You fire it in the same way you might a gun. I've not had much experience past shooting my older brother's air rifle when we were kids, but that doesn't bother me. I'll pick it up. Picking things up is easy.

"Walker? Walker? Come in. Do you read me?"

A little black box crackles to life from within one of the shredded uniforms. Walker. A curiously unimaginative name. He might as well have said his name was Smith if it was anonymity he was after. The colony thrusts out a spindle of jelly and plucks the radio from its nest.

"I read you, Point – nothing here."

Crackle.

"I read you – nothing? Are you sure? Where the fuck did they go?"

"Dunno. Walker out."

The colony's ability to replicate human voice patterns is remarkable. I can't help but be awed by it. Its surface ripples again: *do not concern yourself.* I have no idea how I understand what it is saying, but I do. It's like reading words on a page now.

"What the hell is going on?" Marcus whispers from behind me. In the past, such a sudden enquiry would have made me jump, but not now. I knew he was there. I know where all of them are now. Every single one.

"Don't worry," I say. "Everything's being sorted."

"Sorted?" Marcus sounds incredulous. "What is wrong with you, Meg? What did..." His voice drops down to barely a whisper. "What did that thing do to you?"

Janos is behind him staring at me. What has happened to me? So hard to explain without it sounding like madness. I smile slowly.

"We have a new ally," I say.

"A new... a new ally? That thing? Meg... come on."

"It tested me and found me truthful. It trusts me. We helped liberate it, so it owes us. The collective is back together now, and so it will help us."

"Help us... and then what?" Janos asks.

"It can go home," I say.

"It can go home?"

"Yes."

Well... it's as good a reason as any.

"Oh, dear Lord..." Marcus sounds both awed and revolted, so I turn around. The colony has shrunk in on itself, creating the perfect replica of a man, just as it did to Brendan and me when it was in the tank. Only now, it looks like what I expect is Walker, complete with his uniform. A few moments more and colour blushes its surface, filling in the transparent gaps until the illusion is flawless. The Walker thing then scoops up the remaining crossbow, and stalks away.

The hunt, as they say, is on.

We keep our distance, and only the threat of death by crossbow bolt keeps Marcus quiet. I can tell he doesn't trust the collective, which is stupid – it is helping us, after all – but his fear of the clean up team is even greater. Janos, on the other hand, is as inscrutable as ever. His expression is hard, his body language stiff. Out of the two of them, I know he is the one I'm going to have to watch.

Another shriek punctures the silence, followed by the dull thud of something striking a wall. I scurry up the slope towards the antechamber where our rope dangles. There's a bolt stuck in one of the walls. Well, at least they tried. We burst in to find the replica of Walker busily engulfing another figure. I can't work out if they're male or female, but it doesn't matter. They're dead. In the corner, someone else whimpers – the last of the clean up team, huddled, stinking of piss and terror. I raise my crossbow and pull the trigger. The bolt leaves with a sigh and buries itself into his head with a soft thump. See? I told you it was easy enough.

"Meg!" Marcus is shocked, but I ignore him. How else did he expect this to go down? It's kill or be killed down here – dog eat dog.

"Now what?" Janos asks. The Walker-thing shudders as its body snaps back into its human form. I look at it, and it nods.

"We leave," I say.

"We leave?"

"Yes."

"Simple as that?"

"Yes. The colony doesn't particularly want us to stay – and I don't know about you, but I've had enough of this place."

"For once, I agree," Marcus says, and scrabbles for the rope. Before anyone can stop him, he's halfway up, halfway towards freedom. Janos doesn't move.

"Ladies first?"

The base of my skull buzzes. I don't trust him, but that doesn't matter. He wouldn't dare try anything here. I know the truth of him, and so does the collective. Any false move from him and he's dead.

I shoulder the crossbow and take the rope. Climbing it is a breeze. Now my nerves are calm. I can see it for what it truly is – a straight climb up with no obstacles. Quite why I couldn't see that before, I don't know. I was so ignorant back then. So very ignorant.

Janos follows me, but the collective doesn't. I look down the well – my eyesight really is quite excellent now – and watch as Walker breaks down, liquefies and then forms back into the shapeless blob of matter that the colony prefers. A complication of ripples striate its surface and I know it is not interested in following us. A warm, trickling sensation runs down my spine. It doesn't have to. Not now.

"What are we waiting for?" Marcus asks.

"Absolutely nothing," I say.

All three of us race down to the clean up team's boat. I can't see any evidence of anyone waiting on the opposite shore – yet. They're probably investigating the cave entrance, or something like that, but they will turn up. I pat the weapon that is slung over my shoulder. We will be ready for them.

One thing that does make me feel slightly uncomfortable is that Janos has done exactly the same. He has a crossbow too and I doubt he'd hesitate to use it. On anyone. Must keep an eye on him. A very close eye.

"Okay – how did they operate this thing?" Marcus breaks my chain of thought. He paws at the machine, turning knobs and flicking switches. Janos grunts and hunkers down to investigate. A loud hum springs into being and my head feels like it might explode.

"Turn it off!" I plead, clutching the back of my skull.

"Too loud," Marcus agrees, and Janos turns a dial that lowers its intensity. It is still agonising, but it is bearable. The other two don't seem to be bothered at all.

I hear a sound from the opposite bank. Movement. They heard the hum, and now they're back. I duck down beside the boat. Marcus and Janos look bewildered at first, but they follow my lead nonetheless. Good job – a bolt whizzes through the air and strikes a rock that was directly behind Janos's head only a split second before.

"How do they know it's us and not the clean up team?" Marcus asks.

"Probably because the clean up team would have radioed in," Janos replies. "They aren't taking any chances. I would think that their team was expendable as ours, so they'll shoot just to be safe rather than sorry."

"Jesus fuck – what the hell have we got ourselves involved in?"

"You don't want to know," Janos says.

While the other two are chatting, I peek over the side of the boat. There are two figures, their heads barely visible as they hide behind boulders. I can't really see them, but I can feel them. Their hearts beat wildly, which vibrates through the rock. I inch my crossbow up and over the side of the boat. I don't look. I don't need to look. I know where they are. I make a tiny adjustment to the right and pull the trigger. The bolt sails over the water and takes off the top of the hiding soldier's head. I hear a bark of disgust from the other boulder and feel a thud as the body hits the floor. Now I can only sense one heartbeat, and it's going batshit insane.

"Fucking hell, Megan!" Marcus says. "How did you do that?"

I shrug. What else can I do?

A voice floats over from the opposite bank. Again, I am struck by the complete absence of accent, so carefully orchestrated to promote complete anonymity.

"Stop!"

Hmm. Stop. Interesting.

"We didn't fire the first shot," I reply.

"Megan!" Janos hisses. "Let me deal with this."

Let him deal with this? The traitor? I give him a disgusted look, but shut up nonetheless. If he thinks he can be useful, then great, let him be useful.

"I am standing up," Janos announces, and I cannot help but mark the shift in his own accent. No longer thick and exotic, this is the voice of Janos the Professional. "I have no weapons. Hold your fire."

He raises his hands to show he has nothing in them, and pauses. He takes in a deep breath. I know why – there is every chance the last of the clean up team is going to take his head off the moment he stand up. But, surely, he knows if he did that, I would do the same back?

Janos stands up in one swift, fluid motion. The moment hangs. No one breathes. When no shots are fired, he visibly relaxes.

"Where is everyone?" the voice barks.

"Dead," Janos replies.

"By you?"

"No. By the Entity. It is in there. It can't get out."

Oh, Janos, you pretty little liar, you. Still, if it gets us out of this situation alive, I am not going to contradict you.

"The Entity? It's real?"

"Yes. It is."

"Why did you shoot Mendelsohn?"

"He shot first. It was self defence."

There is a pause.

"Okay."

And that's it. With that one word, we're expected to trust this man. He hasn't offered us his name, and as far as we know, he killed Brendan – he certainly tried to shoot us just now – but we're expected to trust him. It grates against me, barbed wire in my soul, but we have no choice.

Slowly, Marcus and I stand up. I lay my crossbow on the floor before doing so. I don't want to, but I have to play along, be a part of this pantomime. The man opposite doesn't move as we adjust the low-frequency noisemaker and push the boat into the shallows. There is no reaction when we lower it into the water and push off into deeper water.

For the first time in what feels like an age, a prickle of fear plays at the base of my spine. This time, it is far more primal, more instinctual than before. You can reason with another person. Reason means nothing to the reptilian brain of a pliosaur.

I can tell the others are having the same thoughts. Their apprehension makes the boat sing with vibrations. Then another, deeper, larger vibration joins them, separate from the machine that is supposed to keep it at bay. It is too primitive to register true emotion, too simple to have thoughts, but the jerkiness of its movements can only translate into one thing: anger.

I swivel my head slowly from side to side, systematically scanning the surface of the water. There are no ripples, nothing physical to read, but I know it's there. I don't know how, I just do. It was scared off once, repelled by the confusing cacophony. Not this time.

"It's coming," I whisper.

"What? It can't. The machine-"

"Confuses it. That's why it didn't attack last time. This time, it won't be stopped so easily."

As if eager to prove my point, a huge dark shape explodes from our left, sending the boat reeling. Janos fights to save the oars as the pliosaur thrashes around, maddened by the machine. Its vast jaws gape, exposing six inch conical teeth, each one as thick as my wrist. It slaps its flippers down, making us grab the dinghy's gunwale to stop ourselves from being washed overboard.

Then it charges.

Marcus screams like a girl. It's aiming for the source of its confusion, right next to him. I don't wait for impact. Instead, I stand up and dive out the other side of the boat into the freezing water.

I can hear the others shouting my name, but I ignore them. The shore isn't that far away. Behind me, there is a splintering crash and a high-pitched squeal – I can only guess that the low frequency emitter has finally succumbed to the assault. When the hum stops, I feel instantly sharper; my arms fizz, and I am able to power myself through the water with the ease of an Olympic swimmer. I take only one, quick glance behind me to see the pliosaur chomping on the dinghy, Marcus still clinging to it. It throws it up into the air and then slams it back down again to drag it below the waves, Marcus and all.

I guess he was right. He really isn't going to see his family again.

I keep going until I can feel rock under my feet. I stagger out of the water, but I am not shivering. Behind me, I hear more splashing. I glance around. It is Janos. He has also survived. I look past him to the lake's surface. It still boils as the pliosaur finishes off the dinghy – and I guess, Marcus.

Janos gives me what I can only describe as a murderous look.

"You both survived?"

Accent or not, the last remaining member of the clean up team sounds surprised. I'd bet anything he was hoping the pliosaur would take us out.

"Not... all of…us," Janos pants. It is then I realise I am barely breathing hard. "One perished."

The man opposite smiles and whips up his crossbow.

"Wrong."

Janos's eyes widen. His mouth opens in anticipation to speak, but before any entreaty can leave it, the soldier fires. The bolt buries itself into his skull with a spray of blood and brain matter. As if shocked to find itself dead, Janos's body stands to attention before slumping to the floor.

The soldier then turns to me. I smile. The fizz is back in my head and in my arms. I feel the vibration as his finger pulls the trigger. The bolt releases. I sway to one side.

It grazes my ear before burying itself in the rock face behind me.

"What the?" the soldier says.

" 'What the' indeed," I say before I reach out and grasp his neck. He looks pathetically surprised at the turn of events. Inside me, the colony surges forward, giving my grip strength a human should never possess. I crush his windpipe the way a small child might crush a drinking straw. He gurgles and flops at my feet.

Chapter Sixteen

And then there was one (of many).

There's a commotion behind me. The tower, after aeons of lying dormant, is awakening. It doesn't need to be here any more, not now that it has a way out. The colony has their way out. It flickers in and out of vision and in and out of reality. Around me, the rocks shake and I know it is time for me to go.

I pick up the radio that the last man standing carried. His tags declare him as Weimar. Weimar, really? Stupid name. I open my mouth and adjust my jaw, then depress the button.

"Leader to Base, do you read?" I say, in Wiemar's voice.

Immediately, there is a reply.

"Base to Leader, we read. Any news?"

I can't help but smile. Oh, what fun we shall have.

"Yes. No survivors. I am the last. All targets destroyed."

"And the Entity?"

My smile widens.

"Safe and sound. Safe and sound."

Well… you know what they say – if you can't beat them, join them.

Or something like that.

The End

Made in the USA
Lexington, KY
14 May 2014